One Night
in the *Spa*

Kathy Lyons

Previously released on Entangled's Ever After imprint copyrighted August 2013.

Entangled Publishing, LLC
2614 South Timberline Road
Suite 109
Fort Collins, CO 80525
Visit our website at www.entangledpublishing.com.

Brazen is an imprint of Entangled Publishing, LLC. For more information on our titles, visit www.brazenbooks.com.

Edited by Stacy Abrams
Cover design by Heather Howland
Photography by Shutterstock

Manufactured in the United States of America

First Edition August 2013

To Stacy and Liz
You make this fun!
THANK YOU!
And to the real David and Kim,
May your lives be filled with more love
Than can be put on a printed page.

Chapter One

"So I'm trying to bulk up, but without…"

Kim Castillo tried not to strangle her client. He was a middle-aged bodybuilder, a man who'd spent thousands on personal training, and who was currently doing nothing more than asking her advice. It wasn't his fault that she felt as though she was about to crawl out of her own skin. He was droning on about different supplements, shifting into poses to show off his progress.

Can you say midlife crisis? He was a jerk, but he paid well, and damn it, she couldn't stop looking. Not just at his impressive pectorals, but at the guy doing squats a few feet away. There was an adolescent in the corner who had really nice calf muscles, and even the old guy near the cardio machines had broad shoulders. Old, young, athlete, or not—if the body was male, she was looking. And that made her absolutely insane.

That was her. Miss Ogle-the-Weight-Lifters.

It's a medical condition, she reminded herself. There were fancy words for it, even a chart with hormone levels and the like, but it all boiled down to two words: super horny. Yup. That was her: twenty-four years old and suddenly a female horndog.

She ground her back teeth, trying to force herself to focus on her client. Besides, there was nothing new out there for her to see. She was no stranger to the male form. She'd practically grown up in various gyms around Chicagoland, she'd aced all her anatomy classes, and then she'd become a personal trainer while building a pro racquetball career. She knew bodies—male and female. And yet for some reason, completely out of the blue, she abruptly couldn't stop staring at them.

"Kim? Kim, what do you think? Can you see a difference?" Frank Johnson struck another bodybuilder pose, flexing his pecs and bunching his abs. At some point, he'd pulled off his shirt just so he could show off for her. And damn it, he was impressive for a middle-aged guy with a wife, a mortgage, and three kids.

"Very nice," she said, unable to keep the throaty purr from her voice. Where the hell had that come from? "But you need to put on your shirt. We've got a policy on that, and I *am* the manager here."

"Oh. Right," he said as he took his time getting dressed again. "Um, hey, I know you have brochures and stuff on the supplements the club recommends. Do you mind if we go grab a few?"

She blinked. "No problem. I'm sure Danni can—"

"But I want to go over them with you." He flashed her a charming smile. "Do you mind? I'd really appreciate it."

She blinked. It was against the rules to take a member upstairs to the office suite. The club was open until eleven, but the office suite closed at seven and it was now after nine. As manager here, she had to stick to the rules. "Tell you what, I'll grab what we have and bring them down while you shower."

He rubbed a hand over his head and looked rather charming, with the way his pecs bunched as he did it. "Come on, Kim. You've known me for years. I just want to talk to you about them."

She looked at Frank, feeling jittery and lustful all at once. God, she was sick. She just wanted to get home so she could climb the walls there. But then her business mind kicked in. Yes, Frank was a jerk, but one who paid very well. And— bonus—if she made nice with him now, she could probably get him to sign up for the elite training and sports massage package. Sales were sluggish; her job here at John's Fitness depended on that promotion going well. And all of that— the forms and the brochures—were upstairs.

"We just have to make it quick," she said with a smile. "Follow me." She breathed a sigh of relief as they left the main weight room. Her eyes had been roving so much, she'd given herself a headache.

Frank kept talking as she led him up the stairs. Kim tuned him out, her mind already churning over ways to blow off steam. Maybe a sauna. Her knee injury meant she couldn't exercise except for yoga, and frankly, turning herself into a pretzel hadn't worked for her.

She unlocked the door to the office suite, flipping on the light as she went to the bank of filing cabinets. Beyond her were the offices—hers included—completely dark at this late hour. Frank was following a step behind her, gabbing all the way. But at his first pause for breath, she went into her sales pitch.

"You know about the spa attached to the club, right? Pamper Me Spa. Have you thought about our new fitness massage package? It's perfect for elite athletes like— *Ump!*"

Suddenly, Frank had shoved her up against the filing cabinet so hard the breath was knocked from her lungs. Then before she could do more than gasp, he had flattened himself along her back. His hands turned into tentacles, groping her everywhere while his erection started shoving rhythmically against her butt.

She couldn't believe how fast it happened. One second, elite athletics, the next—pinned.

"Frank! Stop!"

"Yeah, baby, show me how you like it," he groaned in her ear.

WTF? Fury pounded in her ears, and she started to move on reflex. She slammed backward with her elbow and stomped hard with one foot. But she was flattened, and worse, he had about a hundred pounds on her. She had little leverage and he was just too damned big.

She was just gathering breath for a really good scream when suddenly, the bastard was off her. She barely registered an *umph* of sound before she was staggering backward, abruptly free of the asshole.

She stumbled then caught herself, her knee suddenly blossoming in pain. She ignored it. Spinning around, she watched in stunned surprise as David—her best friend David, the spa manager from next door—proceeded to pummel her client with lightning-fast rabbit punches.

Damn, he was amazing. She'd never seen fists fly so fast. Frank was a big guy. A really big guy, but David had him down and whimpering like a child. He had the guy pinned with one knee while he kept delivering blow after blow.

She took a ragged breath, telling herself to call security, but she couldn't manage to move. Her legs were too weak, her knee was screaming, and so she stood there staring. Frank was down, she was safe, and David was... Blood was starting to flow—all of it Frank's—and yet the fury she saw in her friend's face wasn't fading.

"David. David! Stop!"

She moved forward and tried to grab his arm. But not only was he fast, damn, he was strong. A lot stronger than she expected.

"David!"

He froze for a second, then rapidly twisted around to look at her. His blue eyes were dark and intense as he scanned her from head to toe. "Are you all right? Did he hurt you?"

She gaped at him. "Hurt me? You were on him like a ton of bricks. He just…" She looked down to the still-whimpering Frank, feeling a surge of satisfaction at the man's battered face. One eye was already closed from swelling, his nose was broken, and he was working his jaw as if it might have popped out of place. But no fractured bones.

She took a deep breath, trying to steady her pounding heart. She had to think. She looked to her best friend, hoping for a little clarity. His sandy-brown hair was wild and his lean body was as taut as a guitar string. And what she saw in his eyes both terrified and reassured her: he was blisteringly furious, all too ready to start pounding on the bastard again.

That made her feel safe. The drama was over.

Not so good was the fact that once Frank recovered some of his equilibrium, he was going to remember that his brother was an attorney. One who could make life uncomfortable for her, the club, and most of all David. Especially since she'd broken the rules in the first place by bringing Frank up here. What an idiot she'd been. And thank God her best friend had been here to save her.

"It's over, David," she said, as much to herself as to him. "Frank was just confused about something, right, Frank?"

The asshole nodded, the motion jerky. He mumbled something like "Sorry," but it was David who gaped at her.

"You don't seriously think—"

She squeezed David's arm, gaining strength from the heat of his skin and the corded power in his biceps. He was here. She was safe. The whole thing was over. "I think," she said, her tone filled with underlying meaning, "that Mr. Johnson behaved inappropriately and that I'm considering calling the cops. And telling his wife."

"I'm really sorry," Frank said through swelling lips. "Big mistake. No need…"

"Your wife?" David pressed. "You know, I think she's scheduled an appointment for tomorrow in the spa—"

"No!" Frank was practically apoplectic.

Kim crossed her arms and glared down at the man. "I'm so sorry, Mr. Johnson," she said drily. "I find we will have to terminate your membership, effective immediately. I'll be writing a full report on this incident, but I suggest you leave now."

The man nodded, though the gesture obviously pained him. Meanwhile, David just glared. His fists were still tight, his biceps impressively bulked, and his teeth were bared.

Damn, she'd never seen her friend looking so fierce. Or so... hot? She never got into the testosterone and blood scene. Never. And yet... Kim swallowed. Suddenly, her best friend in the world was looking like an action star. And she couldn't stop staring.

Sadly, this wasn't the time or place for her to be thinking like that. So she cleared her throat and tried to get a handle on her raging hormones.

"Uh, David," Kim said.

"Yeah?"

"You should probably get off him now. I don't think Mr. Johnson will be causing us any more problems."

David looked down as if surprised that he was still straddling the guy. "Oh. Um, okay." He got up, taking his time and "accidentally" stumbling as he moved. One of his knees dropped straight onto Frank's solar plexus. "Oops," he drawled.

Kim choked back a hysterical laugh. This wasn't a funny situation and she wasn't amused. Her nerves were stretched taut, her illness was making her look at her best friend as if he were a really chiseled bar of expensive chocolate, and... well, there was no *and*. She was insane, and there was nothing else to it. So she turned to the nearest desk phone and hit the number for security. They appeared with gratifying swiftness and ten minutes later, Mr. Frank Johnson was peeling out of the parking lot as if the hounds of hell were on him. And given the way David still seethed, it wasn't a bad decision.

"I hope this doesn't come back to bite us," Kim said as they stood at the door watching Frank drive out.

"I hope he does come back. I'd love a second go at him."

She smiled, the power in her friend's voice steadying her

as nothing else could. It was over. Everything would be fine. "Was it really necessary to destroy his face? He's going to be plotting revenge every time he looks in the mirror."

Normal color was coming back to David's skin. The flush of fury had faded to the light golden tones that were all part of his usual boyish good looks. "Are you kidding? He's lucky I didn't tear off his nuts."

She snorted, another thoroughly inappropriate sound. "I'm glad you didn't. Imagine the paperwork for that."

Then he turned to her, his eyes warming, though the fierceness never left his expression. "Seriously, Kim, are you all right?"

She nodded. "I'm fine. And I could have handled him, you know."

"He's twice your weight and had you pinned. Damn it, you know you can't bring guys into the back office like that. Not alone. Not at night."

She swallowed and ran a shaking hand through her hair. "I know, I know. I've just been so distracted lately. Normally, I would never make a mistake like that."

He grunted, and it wasn't even remotely a nice sound, but she liked it. Apparently, she was way more off-kilter than normal.

They started walking together to the back office. There was no reason for him to follow her, but she was glad of his company.

"God, if I hadn't been there…," he muttered.

She touched his arm. It was a friendly gesture, one that she'd done a thousand times, but this time they both jolted at the contact. Clearly, they were both still hyped up from the adrenaline. "I'm fine," she said firmly, more to herself than to him. "And I would have screamed, you know. Someone would have heard and come running." She took a deep breath, blowing it out as she steadied herself. "Besides, I know a ton of self-defense moves. I do teach that class."

He shuddered, his body actually shaking as he seemed to throw off the horror of what might have happened. In the end, he blew out a long, frustrated breath. "Just…just don't do that again, okay?"

"I won't. I promise." Then she frowned, her mind finally kicking in as she looked around the empty office suite. Mentally, she replayed every moment of the attack. She'd been standing by the filing cabinets, Frank was coming up from behind, and then David had saved her. But he'd saved her from the wrong direction.

She narrowed her eyes. If he'd rushed in from the hallway, she would have heard the door and Frank would have gone flying in the opposite direction. But the men had gone sprawling the other way. Which meant David had come from…her office? But that couldn't be. The office suite had been dark. She was sure of it.

"Why were you here, anyway?" she asked. "I'm grateful, of course, but how did you come to be my knight-errant?"

She watched his eyes widen and he looked away. "Uh… um…"

Now this was the David she knew, the coworker who had been part of every day of her life for the last three years. This floor of the office high-rise had two businesses: John's Fitness and Pamper Me Spa. Though the companies were entirely separate, she and David worked together constantly on joint promotions and the like. There was a pass-through from one business to the other, and members had extra discounts. Add to that their shared love of all things sports, and they'd been best friends from almost the start. And right now, she was seeing the man who had been at her side nearly every day for the past three years. He looked half goofy, half boy-next-door friendly. And right now, he was all embarrassed. "Oh, I smell intrigue!" she said with a laugh. "Come on, Dave, what were you doing?"

"It's, uh, kinda embarrassing."

"Really? Do tell." She leaned back against the desk, her arms folded as she waited for him to answer.

"I, uh, came looking for you."

"I was with a client."

He flashed her an annoyed look. "Yeah, I know. Mr. Bastard Johnson with the tiny—"

"So, we were talking about you?" she interrupted. "In my office?"

"Yeah, well, I was looking for you about an hour ago and then I…well, I fell asleep."

She blinked. "You what?"

"I wanted to talk to you about next week's spa promotion. I was hoping to tie it to a back-to-school theme or something." He shrugged, looking completely embarrassed.

"Don't you have a perfectly good couch in the spa area? Plus recliners and—"

"Yeah, I do, but the cleaning crew's there and it was all quiet back here."

"You just fell asleep? In my chair?"

"On the floor, actually. I decided to wait for you and stretch out my back at the same time. Then the overhead light was buzzing, so I turned it off. And then…"

She snorted. "And then you zonked out. Really, David,

you've been working way too hard if you fell asleep on my office floor."

He sighed. "It was a really long wait. I woke up when I heard you and Bastard—"

"You don't have to keep calling him that."

"Oh, yes I do," he shot back. Then he took a deep breath, and what lovely things that did to his chest. When had David gotten so He-Man buff?

Meanwhile, he was looking down at his shirt, grimacing at the blood splattered there. "Damn," he muttered as he ripped off his spa polo and threw it into the trash. His motions were abrupt and still angry. The suppressed violence of the motion startled her. And gave her a secret thrill. When the hell had her best friend gotten all…manly?

"You could have washed that out," she said, her throat suddenly very dry.

"It's garbage. I don't want anything of that asshole anywhere near you."

She wanted to say something casual. Wanted to stay at the camaraderie of being best friends, but she couldn't. Not with him standing there with his shirt off and his chest rippling with the fury of his motions.

"I'm going to take a shower," he said. "There's a new body wash the spa's promoting that's supposed to give great lather," he said. Then he winked at her. "Imagine me, all covered in girly bubbles." He reached for a towel off a nearby stack, and she watched his abs contract and release, saw the way his delts broadened his shoulders and his biceps bunched with the movement.

She didn't say a word. She couldn't. She was ogling her best friend, and she ought to be ashamed. Instead, she was breaking out in a sweat.

"Kim?" he asked, turning to her.

She blinked, then came back to herself with a start. "Hmm?"

"Nothing. You were…you were staring."

"Oh! Right. Sorry. I, um, I was noticing that you've been working out."

He grinned. "Yeah. I decided all these hard-bodied men were making me look bad."

"You've got nothing to be worried about," she said with absolute truth. A second later, she realized she'd reached up a hand to touch him. Thankfully, she came back to herself in time to snatch it away before they actually connected. "Uh…sorry," she mumbled, her cheeks heating.

"Don't be sorry," he said. "I'm glad you noticed. Not many people do."

She shook her head. "You hide it under those spa shirts." As manager of the spa, he was required to wear a pastel polo that did nothing to accent his manliness. How could she not have noticed before how very…ripped he was? "You've got a swimmer's body," she said, unable to stop herself from staring. "A very nice inverted triangle." Oh hell, her illness was showing again. Quickly, she had to find a way to put them back to normal footing. "You'd, um, kick ass at racquetball if you'd practice a bit more."

She'd been encouraging him to play since the first day they'd met three years ago. She'd been at the height of her pro racquetball career, he'd been the guy who told her why she had chronic pain from the piriformis. Bad hip movement had been the key to her constant pain in the ass. They'd started talking sports injuries then, analyzing every pro player who'd gotten hurt or was about to break down. It had been an easy step from there to watching a few Cubs games together. A few weeks later, he got tickets to a Bears game, then later a Bulls game. Before long, they were sports buddies at every major sporting event Chicagoland had to offer.

"If you ever want some drills—" she continued.

"I think we've already established that no amount of practice will get me to your level of play," he said, all casual friendliness.

That was true enough. He just didn't have the love of racquet sports that she did. Meanwhile, she flashed him a grateful smile. Everything was back to normal, more or less. "So, um, thanks again. For the rescue."

"Not that you needed it," he finished for her.

She bit her lip. "Actually, I probably did. I'm really grateful, David. Come sleep on my floor anytime," she quipped, then abruptly gasped at what she'd half insinuated. Thankfully, he didn't seem to notice her suggestive comment. Instead, he reached out and touched her face, slowly stroking his thumb down her cheekbone.

The caress was so damn intimate, she nearly freaked out. This was her best friend, the guy she bitched to about her ACL surgery and employee problems. And suddenly she was thinking all things pornographic about him. It was wrong! It was just her illness latching onto the nearest male. But David was her best friend and didn't think of her that way. Meanwhile, he was speaking, his expression tortured.

"If you need to talk about what happened—you know, to freak out or de-stress or whatever—I'm here."

She nodded, unable to speak.

"You'll call me, won't you? Day or night. For whatever reason."

She swallowed, and suddenly her gaze canted away. "I will. I promise."

"Kim…," he said, her name coming out half-strangled. She didn't look back at him. She couldn't. She was too afraid she might jump him or something. In the end, his hand dropped away. "Call me, okay?"

"I will," she said as she backed up a step. She needed distance from him. Time to get her insanity under control or she'd screw up everything.

"Okay, change of plans. I'm not going to shower, but I need to go lock up. Don't leave without me. Let me escort you to your car."

She laughed, the sound too high. "Don't be silly. It's a protected garage."

"Even so. Let me be caveman about this, okay?"

"You're being ridiculous."

He just looked at her, silently demanding she agree. In the end, she relented.

"Fine, but hurry up. I've still got to hit a grocery store on the way home."

"Oh, the glamorous life you lead," he drawled.

"Just go," she said.

He nodded, then after a long look, he headed for the office door. "Ten minutes. I swear."

She tried to wait. She really did, but seeing Dave defend her like that had put her into overdrive. He was her best friend. He was the shoulder she cried on when her knee detonated during regionals. He was the one who brought her soup and argued Cubs versus Cards with her. No way would she risk losing that with him just because her hormones were way out of whack. So she took the coward's way out. She scribbled him a quick apology note, grabbed her purse, and left.

Yes, she was running away, but hell, what other choice did she have? She couldn't very well jump her best friend. That would destroy the only stable thing left in her life.

• • •

David Pepke splashed cold water on his face, needing the icy hit to clear his thoughts.

I suck at corporate espionage. That was his primary thought. The rest was just a jumbled mash of emotions, all tied up with Kim, the woman he'd been lusting after for three years now. The very same woman he'd just betrayed by snooping through her computer files.

It had been a simple plan so many years ago. Step 1: establish himself next door as manager of the spa. Step 2: develop the relationship between his business and Kim's club. Then step 3: swoop in and take over everything. In short, he was a corporate raider, but in a very small-business kind of way. In truth, he hadn't even seen that far ahead when he first started working next door. But the end result was the same. If everything went according to plan, then his company would be in charge and—depending on how the restructuring went—Kim could lose her job.

That hadn't felt like a big deal when Kim was the rising star in professional racquetball. But she wasn't rising anymore. A torn ACL had sidelined her, possibly for good. Her job was the only thing she had right now—something she told him often after a couple glasses of wine—and any threat to that was likely to destroy her. He'd seen how on edge she was, and it was getting worse every day. She was distracted, making mistakes, and—God!—she'd let that lecherous bastard upstairs alone with her.

He leaned against the chilly tile wall, barely restraining himself from punching a hole in it. A growl clawed up his throat as he remembered slamming his fist into the bastard's face. If she hadn't stopped him, he might have killed the asshole. Part of him still wanted to.

But at least that dickhead had betrayed her openly. He'd been up-front about his wants, whereas David had been hiding his crush for three years now. He'd been watching her from afar, developing their friendship until she saw him as a brother. And hadn't that been a genius move on his part? Hell.

And then, just when things couldn't get any worse, he'd had to get those files off her computer. He'd sneaked into her office, e-mailed financial files to himself, and then…

He swallowed, forcing himself to deal with his most heinous crime. And then he'd read her private journal. He hadn't meant to, but it had been right there. An open window on her computer that he'd read before even realizing what it was.

Something is very wrong with me.

That was the first line. Something was wrong with Kim. Having seen that, there had been no stopping him from reading further.

I knew this was going to be hard. No one ends a pro career without some amount of change. But this? This is making me insane, and I don't have anyone I can talk to about it. All my friends are here at work. What am I going to do?

He'd stared at that entry for a very long time. It was one

thing to accidentally see something on her screen. It was another to go paging back through her journal. But she sounded desperate. And besides, he'd already ventured into corporate espionage. How much worse was snooping through her private thoughts?

A lot. But he'd done it anyway. He flipped back a month and started skimming. He read all about her ACL tear. Her knee was toast and that ended her career. There was the usual anger and bitterness, but no one loses a sport without that. And she'd been one of the best.

Worse, her best chance medically was to completely rest her knee. That meant no activity. No teaching fitness classes, no private racquetball lessons. Nothing. For a woman who'd spent ten hours a day in highly physical activities, the complete lack of any exercise was going to make her antsy, to say the least.

I can't stop looking at the men. It makes no sense. Big ones, fat ones, lean ones, and oh God, those hard-bodied ones? It's ridiculous, but I really think something is seriously wrong with me.

He'd read that entry twice, his mind churning. Was it possible? Didn't she understand anything about her own body? That once the daily regimen of constant training ended, all sorts of denied urges started pushing to the fore. Sexuality being one of the first. Especially in a twenty-four-year-old, otherwise healthy woman.

He'd been still staring at that entry, trying to figure out what to do about it, when Kim and the asshole had come into the office suite. And then his attention shifted, the asshole attacked, and he'd burst out of her office as though he was Batman.

He didn't regret it. Hell no! But now he was up shit's creek without a paddle. He knew all these things about Kim, knew she was in trouble emotionally, but he had no way to tell her how he'd found the information.

He should just admit to the truth. He should confess everything and let the chips fall where they may. It was time he stopped being a coward anyway. He needed to man up and just tell her how he felt. Except there was all this corporate crap in the way. Negotiations were touchy, someone was lying—hence the financial research on her computer—and this was just not the time for her to find out bad stuff about him. How did he tell her in one breath that he'd been in love with her for years, then in the next confess to betraying her professionally?

He sighed and let his head drop against a cabinet wall. It didn't matter how hard it was going to be. It didn't matter if she hated him forever. He had to man up. He had to tell her what was going on—for her sake, not his. She was in trouble. She thought she was *insane*. He had to talk to her.

He slammed off the water and closed up in record time. Five minutes later, he was crumpling up her note in his fist and cursing like a sailor. She'd left.

Well, fuck that. Tonight was not the time for her to be alone.

Chapter Two

David knocked on her apartment door while simultaneously trying to calm the rapid beat of his heart. There was no reason to panic. So Kim had bolted at the first opportunity— after being assaulted. So she thought she was insane or sick or something. There was no reason to be worried about her. She was fine. Hadn't she said so in her note?

It was all bullshit, and they both knew it. Just as she had to know he wasn't leaving until he could talk to her.

He knocked again.

"Open up, Kim. It's me." He waited, his worry for her growing by the second. After another minute with no response, he banged again and this time pitched his voice loud enough to disturb the neighbors. "Come on, Kim. I'm worried sick here, so you might as well open up."

"I'm fine," came her muffled voice. "Can't we just talk about it tomorrow?"

"No. Now open up."

He heard her curse, then slide the bolt. But when the knob finally turned, she didn't open the door more than the chain allowed. "You're a pain in the ass, you know that, Pepke?" She always called him by his last name when she was pissed at him.

"Right back at ya, Castillo. Now open up."

She cursed again—words he'd never heard her utter before—and slammed the door shut. He was about to start pounding when he heard the chain slide. A moment later, her door opened and she was walking away from him.

She wore tight yoga pants that hugged her trim ass in lust-inducing silky black. Above was a yoga top, the thin crisscross straps doing little to support her bouncing breasts. Oh shit, his blood had just left his brain to parts south.

Meanwhile, she sauntered through her tiny apartment, kicked the yoga mat aside with surprising fury, then dropped down onto her couch. Then with a hard glare at him, she grabbed a pint of Cherry Garcia ice cream and dug in.

"I'm fine," she repeated sullenly. "You can see I'm fine, so go away."

He didn't argue with her. Instead, he quietly shut the door behind him and looked about the small apartment. Usually the woman was neat as a pin, almost on the anal side about her environment. Not so now. The place looked like the men's locker room on a really bad tournament weekend. There were clothes everywhere, half-eaten food, and even more bizarre, partially done craft projects scattered about. He saw a jigsaw puzzle, a bad attempt at crochet, and something that looked like it ought to be string art but was more like tiny nails banged haphazardly into a piece of wood.

"Yes, I can see that everything's just peachy," he said as

he closed the box on a half-eaten pizza. "Gone on a junk-food binge, have we?"

She stabbed her spoon into the ice cream and scooped up a massive bite. "What makes you say that?" she asked, her tone heavy on the sarcasm.

He gestured at the crumpled-up yoga mat. "What happened to your Evening De-Stress ritual?"

"It's been supplanted by my new best friends: Ben and Jerry." She lifted the pint of ice cream in case he missed the reference. He hadn't. After all, he had sisters. He knew what chocolate and ice cream meant. It signaled: woman in a mood. All men steer clear.

Apparently, he wasn't smart enough to do that. Taking a swift turn to the kitchen, he grabbed a spoon for himself, trying not to notice the pile of dirty dishes in the sink, on the counter, and even in the microwave. Crap, she was in total meltdown.

Then he looked at the bookshelf between kitchen and living room. The other shelves were in disarray, but the top one remained pristine. Her family photos, most especially one of her and her father in their Sunday best. It was the last picture she had of him before he'd died when she was eleven. If that area had been screwed up, he would be thinking mental hospital for sure. Fortunately, this area was still clean. Which told him she was freaking out, but not a danger to herself.

"Move over," he said as he crossed back into the living room. Then when she didn't accommodate him, he squeezed in anyway. After all, he had no problem if she was going to be draped on top of him. But apparently she did, because she huffed angrily, then shoved the entire pint at him.

"Take it. I was done anyway."

He looked into the empty container. "Apparently so."

She stood up, took two steps, then stopped in the middle of her living room. Soothing ocean waves were playing over the speakers and she abruptly cursed, grabbed her iPod, and stabbed it off.

"Don't like the ocean?" he asked, pitching his voice calm despite his growing panic. He'd never seen her so indecisive. As if she didn't know what to do with herself.

"You know I do," she snapped.

"But the waves—"

"Are pissing me off." Then for emphasis, she blew out a raspberry candle. Apparently, her favorite scent was annoying her too. God, things were looking worse and worse.

He set aside the empty pint, then grimly crossed his arms. "So, do you want to keep going insane or are you going to start talking to me?"

"Goddamn it, David—"

"If you say you're fine one more time, I'm going to throw you over my knee and spank you."

"As if you could," she taunted.

"You know I can," he shot back. He'd done his share of wrestling as a kid. Against her, he had the height and weight advantage, and a growing need to put his hands on her. Hell yes, he could best her.

Apparently, she knew it too. So with another angry huff, she dropped down in the chair diagonal to the couch. Then she folded her arms and glared at her drooping plant in the corner.

He sighed. "Kim—"

"I'm sick, okay? Like seriously sick. I've seen a doctor.

It's all under control, but…but it's taking me some time to adjust."

His blood ran cold and he abruptly leaned forward. "You're sick?"

"It's no big deal."

He threw his hands up on the air. "Criminy, you're like talking to a parrot. It's no big deal. I'm fine. Bull-fucking-shit, Kim."

Her gaze shifted to him. "Criminy? Where the hell did you learn that?"

He flopped back onto the couch. "Really? You're going to start asking me about my swear words?"

"It's from, like, the 1800s."

"It's from my friend's aunt Tilde, okay? It's one of her favorite words. Have no idea what it means. Don't even know how to spell it. Now for the love of God, will you tell me what's wrong with you?"

"I'm *developing*!"

He stared at her. He looked at her, replayed the conversation in his brain, and still didn't get it. What the hell did "developing" mean? "Um—"

"I'm going through puberty, okay? I've suddenly got real periods, I've gained like a hundred pounds, and these things won't stop!" She gestured to her breasts. Come to think of it, they were fuller than he remembered. Beautifully so.

"Um, Kim. Aren't you twenty-four?"

"And a half. Yes."

"So didn't you—"

"Go through puberty eons ago? Yeah, that's what I thought. But think about my life for the last decade. I was working out six, eight, sometimes ten hours a day. It wasn't just the racquetball training. I was teaching aerobics classes, self-defense, and lifting weights too. Add to that my school schedule, and I've never had more than fifteen percent body fat. Apparently, that's not enough to develop into a full woman."

He nodded slowly, processing her words. It aligned pretty clearly with what he had already guessed. Given her knee injury, she'd suddenly stopped most of her activity. Her body had finally had a chance to rest, put on some fat, and get back on track in the propagation-of-the-species way. It all made sense.

So why did she say she was sick? Why did she write in her journal that she was insane?

"Kim—"

"Look, my doctor says it's normal—and let me tell you, that was one conversation I never want to have again—but it's just driving me insane. Everything's accelerated, apparently. More intense because I'm so late doing this. But until my hormones balance out and…whatever…I have trouble focusing. I'm antsy and irritable and…and…"

"Horny?"

Her skin flushed a bright red and she suddenly dropped her head into her hands. "Kill me now," she moaned.

He laughed. What would it be like to be going along in what you thought was a normal adult life, then suddenly lose your career and get hit with *puberty* all at once? Not only did she have all this grief about racquetball, but suddenly her hormones were throwing her emotions around like a Ping-Pong ball. No wonder she thought she was going insane.

He exhaled loudly, feeling his tension drain away. "Well, that's a relief. At least I know you're not dying of a brain tumor or something."

She lifted her head to glare at him. "So glad I could help."

He smiled at her. "Come on, Kim. You've got to see the humor in this. I've always envied how together you are—so cool under pressure, unstoppable on the court, driven at work. Hell, I have no idea how you managed to train and go to school at the same time."

"By being focused."

"Well, yeah. It's easy to be focused when you don't have adolescent *distractions* hitting you all the time. You basically grew up in a hormonal monastery and now—"

"I'm stepping onto a porn set."

He knew she was joking. He knew it, and yet his belly tightened up as his stomach sank to his heels. The image of her shaking her stuff and moaning in orgasm during an orgy had him nearly choking on his combined lust and horror.

"Oh my God, Pepke, you should see your face." She threw a pillow at him. "I'm not actually doing a porn show."

"I didn't think—"

"Sure you didn't. You just got sickly pale there for no reason at all." She flopped back into her chair. "I meant that everywhere I look, all I can think about is sex, sex, sex. Is this what is wrong with all those teenagers? It's a wonder they can sit through a class. I can barely sit at my desk for two minutes before I have to be up and doing something. But God forbid I walk into the weight room or the training studio. All those…" She choked off her words.

"Hot, sweaty men?"

"They don't even have to be hot, David. I'm seeing *everything* and *everyone*."

She made it sound as though she was depraved. She certainly looked as if she'd rather die than admit this to anyone, but he was still trying to process the details.

"You mean you've never gone through adolescence at all?" That couldn't be true. She had breasts and hips. Granted, they were curvier now than before, but she had to have gone through some sort of puberty. Right?

She sighed, the sound mournful. "Well, that's what I thought too. And yes, I've had periods and stuff, but they were always light, never regular. And they'd stop altogether during tournament season."

Okay, so she'd been slowed, not stopped. "But you've had boyfriends. I've seen you date."

She nodded. "And I did." She started listing off the men he'd had burned into his brain years before. Brian, Danny, and Bastard Rick—the one who had pushed for more in their relationship, so she'd just dumped him. Flat-out told him to fuck off. Never spoke to him again.

The men lined up in his brain and he realized that she'd never spoken about them with any kind of passion. Just a casual kind of he-and-I-used-to-hang-out way. She'd made it sound as though they'd barely been a blip on her radar. Now he knew why. She'd been dating more because that's what people did, not because she had any true interest in it.

He nodded slowly, his mind finally processing what had happened. "All your time was spent at school or training." Until a little over ten months ago when she'd blown her knee. Then there'd been surgery and three months in a cast and now…and now her body was making up for lost time.

She pushed out of her chair to pace around the room. "Look, I haven't been like a monk or anything. I've kissed.

I've had sex…sort of."

"But you never got into it?" he asked.

"Not like everyone else did. I just never understood what the big deal was."

He felt his lips curve at that. Boy, was she in for a change in perspective. "So are you figuring it out now?"

"Yeah," she ground out. "And it sucks!" She stopped pacing, closed her eyes and let her head drop back with an anguished moan. It was a pose of defeat, and yet he couldn't help but see every line over her curvaceous body. She'd been too thin before, too much like a marathon runner with no body fat, minimal curves, and no chest to speak of. Now she was bursting out of her yoga gear, and it was all he could do not to throw her over his shoulder and drag her back to his caveman bedroom.

Then she turned her head to stare at him. "What are you grinning at?"

He tried to wipe the smile off his face, but he couldn't quite do it. It was terrible of him—she was really struggling here—but all he could think was: no wonder. No wonder he was just her sports buddy. It was because her body had been shut down. Her female urges had been locked away, but not any more. Finally, he could relate to her as a man who wants a woman.

Hallelujah!

Except he had to tread carefully. After all, any Tom, Dick, or Harry could sexually overwhelm a woman, especially one as confused as she was right then. But he didn't want to overwhelm her. He wanted to seduce her correctly, show her the delights of sexuality in the right way. He wanted to *love* her, and that took a delicate hand.

And the first step—damn it—was to be completely non-sexual with her. He had to remind her that they were friends. Get her back to a sense of security and calmness inside her changing body. Only then could he take the next step.

Patience was key, but hell, that was hard to come by when the woman was standing there in a yoga top with her nipples pointed and her body all lush and curvy. He had to do this right, but it was going to be hard to go slow.

"What?" she demanded, her tone half-hysterical. "You're staring. And thinking. I can always tell when you're thinking, and that makes me nervous."

"Afraid you're going to bet me on the Bulls again and you'll lose another two hundred dollars?"

She waved her fingers at him. "Pfft. You've got no Chicago pride. Never have."

"What I've got is two hundred of your dollars."

"Yeah, well, we're in football season now and you haven't got a prayer."

He snorted. "Bring it, dollface."

She stuck her tongue out at him.

He laughed.

And just like that, equilibrium was restored.

Five minutes later, she pulled out her laptop, and they started discussing their fantasy football picks. Just like normal.

Except that every spare brain cell he had was busy plotting her sexual awakening.

His opportunity came sooner than he expected. An hour into heated fantasy football debate, and suddenly they both were pointing at a web page of statistics. He was arguing that numbers were all that mattered in fantasy games. She was saying that any game that ignored reality in favor of abstracted numbers was ridiculous.

She was fierce as she squared off nose-to-nose with him. "Any game that puts Carson Palmer as a better quarterback than Ben Roethlisberger is a stupid-ass game!"

He had a retort to that. Something about how she just didn't understand the lure of stats, when suddenly they were close enough to kiss.

He saw her breath catch and her eyes go wide. Her gaze suddenly dropped to his mouth and she licked her lips. He knew what she was thinking because he was thinking it too. Or picturing it: the two of them naked and writhing while he thrust hard and fast into her.

Except, of course, he wasn't sure she was thinking *that* exactly. Only that she was licking her lips, and he'd waited three long years for this moment.

So he seized it. He kissed her. He just pressed forward and started moving his lips over hers.

She gasped, obviously surprised, but she didn't move away. In fact, a split second later, she was pushing harder against him.

He angled his mouth over hers, he thrust with his tongue, and he reached out a hand to touch her face.

He felt her shiver when he connected with her skin. They were pressed thigh to thigh, so he knew it when she tensed all over, then suddenly went liquid. She melted into him, and he wasted no time.

His other arm came around her waist as he moved over her on the couch. Slowly, he pushed her backward, never breaking the seal of their mouths. He couldn't as she began to duel with him.

He was thrusting into her mouth, his blood overheating

in a flat second. Then she moaned something that his dick took to mean *yes! Right now!*

He slid his hand to the back of her head, feeling the silky weight of her hair against his hand. It was sweet, but there was no time to appreciate it. Her hands were suddenly on his shirt. She gripped it, hauling him closer.

Not a problem there. She was practically lying flat out on the couch, so now he pressed down on top. God, she felt so good. Womanly and wild. Her body was moving against him in irregular, uncontrolled need. Her hands were alternately clenching in his shirt and digging into his chest. And her kiss was insane with frenzy. She pushed, she sucked, she twisted.

Then suddenly, she shoved him away. Hard.

And she was a strong woman.

One second, he'd been on top of her just trying to keep up. The next, she'd all but thrown him to the ground. She didn't have full leverage, but she sure as hell had enough strength to make him stumble against the coffee table. Her laptop was saved by sheer luck.

"No!" she rasped. Her word was loud and harsh, her breath coming in rapid pants.

"It's okay," he said, the words reflex more than thought. He was still trying to get his legs under him so he didn't flatten her laptop. "I went too fast. My fault. I—"

"No!" she all but wailed. "God, it's me. I'm so sorry."

Oh, no. His stomach knotted in dread. Anything but the apology. "Kim, it's okay."

"No, it's not. I'm insane!" She dropped her head into her forearms as she curled into a fetal ball on the couch. He reached out to touch her shoulder, but she flinched. "God, I'm so sorry."

"It's okay. We just got a little carried away. It happens."

"No, it doesn't." Her voice was muffled against her arms. "Not to me, it doesn't."

He didn't waste his breath telling her that it did now. That she did have those feelings now, and he was fine with them. That he *wanted* them.

But clearly she wasn't ready to go there yet. And he'd pushed things too fast. Damn, this was going to be a lot harder than he thought.

"Kim, please don't apologize." She didn't answer. "Will you look at me? Please?"

She dropped her arm enough to peer balefully at him. One beautiful brown eye stared mournfully at him. "You don't understand," she said softly.

"I think I do—"

"No!" She shoved up until she faced him eye to eye. "Only two things are normal in my life. My job and you. That's it. Everything else has gone insane."

"But—"

"No buts! I won't do this to you. I won't let us change. You're my best friend, and I'm not screwing that up."

"But what if—"

"I. Won't!"

He shut his mouth. There was nothing he could say to that. She was fiercely determined right now. He could see how adamant she was in her clenched jaw, her narrowed eyes, and the way she fisted her hands in her lap. She wasn't going to let herself get sexually attracted to him. It would be like losing one more piece of her sanity, and she couldn't face that right then.

Well, hell. Only one thing to do. He was her best friend,

after all. She was lost and confused. He wasn't going to make it worse for her. He couldn't.

So he sat down on the coffee table and dropped his arms across his erection to hide it from her. "You're not going to lose me, Kim. I'm your friend."

She nodded slowly. "I know, but—"

"But nothing. I'm not going anywhere."

She looked at him then. He felt as if she studied every millimeter of his face. He kept his expression as bland and reassuring as possible.

"Okay," she finally said. Then she looked away. "It's late, David, and it's been a really, um, eventful day. I've bared my soul to you and you've made horrible fantasy football picks."

"As if—"

"Can we talk more tomorrow?"

He cut off his next words and substituted the ones she wanted to hear. "Of course." He stood up, doing his best to shield her view of his crotch. She'd probably freak if she knew how rock-hard he was.

But before he made it to the door, he tried one last time. "You can always count on me. You know that, right? I'll always be here for you if you need me."

She flashed him a wan smile. "I know," she said softly. "You're my rock. That's why I'm just going to keep myself hidden away until all this stabilizes. Even best friends get sick of each other sometimes."

"I'm not going—"

"It's a medical condition, David. I just need some time to get my act together."

She wasn't going to listen. And she sure as hell wasn't going to let him in right now. So he gave her the distance she needed. But that was akin to giving her time to shore up her defenses against him again.

Hell.

But that's what she wanted, so he gave her a nod and let himself out of her apartment. But he wasn't giving her long, he decided. In fact, by the time he made it to his car, he had a whole new battle plan in mind.

Chapter Three

David thrust the heavy weight bar up, then dropped it on the metal frame with a *clang*. He wasn't quite done with his reps, but he had to do something to cover his growing erection. *She* had walked in the room, and his body's reaction was immediate. But he had a plan now, he reminded himself. He'd waited a week to implement it, though memories of their kiss tortured him nightly. And now—finally—it was almost time to get started. First he was going to deal with her frustration. That was task 1. He was going to help her past that sexual-need phase before she found someone else to teach her how to do it.

She'd scheduled a facial for tonight. He'd used the excuse of a heavy workload to slide the session to after closing when they'd have the building to themselves. He was going to use the time tonight to talk about her body and her needs. And if that led her to want his help with the problem, then he was more than ready to assist.

Task 2 was the confession about him stealing her computer files. That would be harder to broach, but he needed to get it out there. If nothing else, they were friends. He hoped she'd be able to listen to his reasons and forgive him.

But first he had to relieve her stress. After all, no one could think rationally when everything in her was hot and bothered. He should know. He'd been in that state around her for three long years.

Thankfully, his restraint was about to pay off. And in the meantime, he'd put a lot of thought into exactly how he was going to rev her up before he got his hands on her. That started with him working out in front of her.

"Need a spot?" she asked as she walked over. He forced a casual smile, but inside he was grinning. Her tone might be even, but her gaze lingered on his torso and she'd just unconsciously licked her lips.

"Thanks," he said. He was lying down on the bench, a bar suspended over his chest as he did presses at a rather impressive weight. It was actually too much for him, but tonight was about seduction, so it was worth the extra pain. Meanwhile, she came to stand behind him such that he was looking right up into her face. And if he tilted his head back just a bit, he got a good look at her erect nipples and her delectable groin.

"Any time now, David."

He blinked. Hell, he'd gotten so busy looking he hadn't remembered that he was supposed to be impressing her with his strength. "Right." He put his hands on the bar and thrust upward. It was a struggle. He'd been working out for nearly an hour now, waiting for her to show up.

"Push, David. You've got this. Just…thrust."

She flashed him a mischievous smile. The double entendre was an old joke among lifters. She was teasing him, but damn if the idea didn't work. All he had to do was picture himself thrusting into her, and wham, he had power to spare.

"Ooh! That's good," she said as she kept her hands poised to catch the weight if it fell. It didn't. Not with her murmuring those kinds of encouragements. And not with the way their eyes had caught and held in the mirror.

"Excuse me. Could you help me next, please?"

Both of them jolted as they turned to look at the adolescent poser next to the free weight stack. Jerk. The kid just wanted to ogle her while she watched him lift heavy things. Of course, Dave would have more right to gripe if he hadn't just done the same thing.

"Uh, in a minute," Kim said. At least she sounded as annoyed as he felt.

But the kid had a right to ask for help, and it was her job to do it. So David bit back his sharp retort and reminded himself that he'd have her all to himself in an hour. "Go ahead," he said. "I'm done anyway." He dropped his voice to a low murmur. "I'll send Scott in here to keep an eye on things."

Kim flashed him a look—half-annoyed, half-amused. "I'm fine. We're in an open area, there's other staff around, and besides…" She winked at him. "I can take this kid."

She probably could, but that didn't prevent him from keeping a watchful eye on her. Or from making sure that Scott was nearby before he left to shower.

"See you tonight," he said as he left.

"Yeah," she echoed, though her voice sounded pensive. "About an hour."

. . .

Kim watched David walk away, his swimmer's body lean and graceful as he moved. God, he was gorgeous. How had she not seen that before?

Lord, her problem was getting worse. Since that night a week ago, she'd been haunted by images of David with his shirt off, David pummeling Frank, David hot and sweaty standing next to her. And that kiss. Holy hell, she'd done little else but fantasize about that kiss…and what might have happened if she hadn't panicked. He was her best friend, and yet she couldn't stop thinking about his body. And his hands all over her body.

But she was not, not, not going to get involved with David. Over the past week, she'd been reminded of how unfailingly kind the man was. Calling Scott to look over her while he was showering was only one of the little things he did for her. She was constantly finding him cleaning up in areas he wasn't technically supposed to be. Hell, he didn't even work here. He managed the adjoining spa—a completely different company—but he was constantly hanging around her gym offering his help. If she didn't know him so well, she'd start to wonder if he was finding excuses just to be around her. Who poked around a business so much if it wasn't his responsibility? Apparently, David did.

He even brought her a smoothie after staff meetings, knowing how much the weekly event stressed her out. Her boss, John, was a jerk of the first order. Mean, miserly, and a lech to boot. He spent half their meetings raking her over the coals for every dime she spent and the other half staring at her breasts. But as soon as John left the building, David appeared at her office door. He had a smoothie in one hand and a sympathetic smile on his face.

In short, he was a good friend, and she wouldn't do anything to jeopardize that. Not even if she wanted him in every way it was possible to want a man.

She considered canceling her facial. She wasn't at all sure that she could remain impassive while he touched her face. Her current insanity had her hyperaware of even the most casual of David's touches. But he'd been so considerate, staying after closing. He said it was because his schedule was too busy, but she knew it was so he could go over their allotted time. He wasn't going to cut her facial short just because he had another client coming in afterward. And as it was an awesome gift—a present to senior fitness staff from the owner of the spa—she really didn't want to give it up.

So, tonight's plan was to be A) professional, and B) friendly. Nothing more. But first she had to finish with the teenager and then close up the club. It took her a while, and she spent the whole of it repeating her mantra: professional and friendly, professional and friendly. By the time she'd locked the doors, killed the lights, and crossed into the spa, she felt content with her decision.

Until she walked into the room where she'd be getting her relaxation package.Somehow David had found raspberry candles. Or maybe it was oil, she didn't know. Either way, the sweet scent enveloped her at the same moment the dim light eased the strain on her eyes. Truthfully, she hadn't even realized that her eyes were hurting until she'd walked in and they'd all but sighed their relief.

The room was relatively small. Not much more space

than the table and sink nearby. But there was a cozy nook for her clothing and David standing at the sink looking all lean and gorgeous.

And naked.

She almost swallowed her tongue until she realized that he was just shirtless. A pair of loose sweats hung low on his very narrow hips. The flickering candlelight cast him in a golden hue—perfect complement to his light tan—and emphasized the hills and valleys of his pecs, and the cut of those mega-hot muscles that outlined... Well, really, she shouldn't be looking there.

"Hey Kim," he said as he flashed her a smile. She looked into the face of her best friend and felt her whole body relax. His eyes were the same sweet blue they'd always been, his smile was friendly, and his tousled hair looked adorably rumpled. "I hope you don't mind. Since it's just us, I thought I'd ditch the uniform. And since it's kinda warm in the room..." He shrugged, causing all sorts of beautiful things to happen along his chest. "If it makes you uncomfortable, I'll go grab a spa polo." He made it sound as if he'd be putting sandpaper on his skin. "Or at a minimum, I can put on a tee."

She smiled. No way did she want him covering up. Just because she'd resolved to maintain their easy friendship didn't mean she had to *think* like a nun. Why cover the scenery?

"Nah, you look great. I can't get over how...um...fit you look."

He grinned. "Like it?" He mock-pumped his arms like a power lifter. He meant it as a joke, but she knew bodies—lifters and layabouts. His was definitely in the perfect category: fit enough to look awesome without the bulk of the steroid freaks.

She leaned back against the doorframe, folded her arms, and gave in to the need to tease. "It worked," she drawled, her expression appreciative. "I had no idea until last week. Makes me feel stupid for being so unobservant."

He straightened with a sigh. "That's my problem in a nutshell. *No one* seems to realize that I'm a guy."

She blinked, hearing an underlying message there. This was old territory for them. He constantly complained that everyone in the building treated him as a buddy. That there was no way he could compete against all those testosterone freaks. But for the first time, she wondered if his words were meant for her. Was he complaining that *she* only treated him as a buddy? And that she had for a very long time? Before now, the idea hadn't even registered. But one kiss, and suddenly everything was different. "I know you're a guy," she said slowly.

"A *heterosexual* guy. They all think, since I manage the spa, that I'm gay." He dropped his hands on his hips, and damn if she didn't notice just how lean he was. Twelve percent body fat at most. "I'm not gay, Kim. I'm very much *not* gay."

"I know," she said, trying to quell the butterflies in her stomach. Was he telling her he wanted to take their relationship to the next level? Well, duh. Of course he was, but she just couldn't go there. Not with him. Even if her nightly fantasies said something entirely different.

So she straightened off the wall and forced herself to speak in a neutral tone. "I really want to thank you for everything you've been doing this last week. You should know I've noticed how sweet you've been. This week and for the last three years. You're even doing this facial after hours. It's so late, I can't believe—"

"I've got nothing to go home to. I even remembered to water my plants yesterday, so no one's going to miss me."

She tilted her head and looked at him. "Why is that, David? You're..." Gorgeous, sexy, sweet, *hot*. "A really nice guy. Why don't you have women lined up for you?" They'd never really talked about this before. Sure, he'd dated a couple times, but nothing serious. And she'd never even noticed before. God, just how oblivious had she been?

"Please," he drawled. "I've got women making appointments to see me." It was a spa joke, and she gave him the obligatory smile. But then he sobered. "The truth is, I don't want just any woman. I want someone who's kind and intelligent. Someone who makes me laugh and who will understand if I'm working too damn hard. Someone who will be there for me during the good and the bad."

She sighed. "Guess we're alike in that."

He didn't say anything and they shared a moment of equal loneliness. Up until her injury, she'd been too busy to be lonely. But now? Hell, the hours just dragged by. Add in her new sexual awareness, and suddenly every minute seemed steeped in unfulfilled desires. But she didn't want to think about her own problems; she was more interested in reinforcing her friendship with David. He was watching her carefully—quietly—and she suddenly wished she could read his mind.

"Who was it?" she asked, startled that she didn't know. They'd been friends for three years, but somehow the talk had remained more about her and less about him. "Who broke your heart?"

He shrugged, then looked at the ceiling. "The usual

suspects, I suppose." He started counting them off on his fingers. "I've had a high school sweetheart, a summer romance, and a college brainiac with breasts…" He flushed and dropped his hands. "Well, let's just say she had lots of assets."

"Why didn't they work out?"

"Couldn't understand fantasy football," he quipped. Then again, he saw she was serious and answered honestly. "Different life goals. The brainiac couldn't understand the whole aesthetician/spa thing."

Kim's eyebrows rose. "What, she thought you were gay?"

He laughed. "No, she knew I wasn't gay. But she couldn't understand how I could enjoy this."

Neither did Kim, really. "Sure, who wouldn't enjoy the long hours, the smelly lotions, the women who demand pampering when you know damn well that whatever you do will never be enough."

He laughed. "Put like that, I guess I don't understand it, either." Then he took a step closer to her, though the cushioned spa bed remained between them. "I like people, Kim. But most of all, I like women. I like making them happy, and I like helping them be as beautiful as they can be. I know it doesn't make sense to most people, but I like working in the beauty industry. Even though—"

"You're not gay. Yeah, I got that part. In fact, in three years I don't think I've ever thought you *were* gay." She said it with a smile, which he returned a thousandfold.

"Speaking of which, I think it's about time you got ready to be pampered."

She nodded, but a surprising bit of tension kept the expression tentative. "Right. Pampering."

He started to step toward her, but stopped himself. It

was as if he wanted to touch her, but held himself back for some reason. "Look, Kim, I know this is rare for you. I know deep down, this is hard."

"What's hard about letting someone pamper you?" She spoke casually, but it was all bravado. She was nervous. Even though this was a spa treatment—and an expensive one at that—she couldn't shake the feeling that she was exposing herself somehow. As if the minute she let her guard down—even for a facial—her lust would leap up and ruin everything.

It was ridiculous. She was in control. But the fear was also very real. And God bless him, David seemed to understand.

"It is hard," he said gently. "But I swear to you, it'll only be about pleasure. About you relaxing and letting your tension go. About having no responsibilities, nothing to do, and no one to please. I'm going to do that for you."

"David—"

"I am. Because that's my job. And even more than that, it's what you need."

She felt hunger stir in her belly with a raw kind of pain. He'd just said exactly what she needed in a way that made her whole body respond. For the next two hours there would be no demands, no responsibilities. This wasn't even on her dime, so all she had to do was relax and enjoy. If he weren't her best friend, she'd jump him right then and there.

His voice was gentle. "It's harder than you thought, isn't it?"

She bit her lip and looked away. He had no idea how hard it was for her to keep her lust under control. "Yeah," she whispered. "Am I completely pathetic?"

"No. You're just a little lost. Everything up until now

has been in service to being a pro athlete. Now that's gone and you're at loose ends. Add in the other change and you're frightened, disoriented, and yet still grieving your career." This time he did touch her. He moved past the spa table to give her a friendly stroke that she felt sizzle all the way down to her toes. "It takes time to find a new way to live. But for tonight, you're going to take a break from all of that. Tonight is just going to be about pleasure."

"You know," she said slowly, "you really are good at this."

He flushed, and wasn't that interesting to see the color creep down his chest? "I really do want the best for you, Kim."

"I know. And, by the way, don't think I don't know the truth."

He jerked slightly, his eyes widening. "Truth? About what?"

"About you, David Pepke." She straightened off the wall, tightening the distance between them even though she knew she shouldn't. It was too risky given her current state of arousal. Sweaty palms, pounding heart, hard nipples. But it wasn't real, she reminded herself. Just hormones. And David was her best friend. She wouldn't risk their friendship just because her body was in overdrive. He was the only thing keeping her from going insane.

"About what?" he prompted when she'd obviously been quiet too long.

"About you being a nice guy. You spend every day pleasing everyone else, making sure everything runs smoothly. Yes, you enjoy it, but it's got to take its toll."

He let out a laugh that sounded relieved. "Oh! Well, tell you what: tomorrow you can give me a facial and massage. But tonight is all about you."

She smiled. "Okay with me. The tonight part, at least. Trust me, you do not want any type of facial I could give!"

"You'd be surprised what I might want," he drawled. Then before she could ask, he quickly held up a spa towel wrap. "I know you've never had a facial before, so here's the drill," he said, affecting a businesslike tone. "I'm going to step out while you undress. It would be ideal if you took off everything, but if you're more comfortable in underwear, that's fine by me. Then wrap yourself in this, lie down, and prepare to be treated like a queen."

"Wow, just a queen? Not a goddess?"

He winked as he slipped past her toward the door. "Well, okay. But only because I like you. One goddess treatment coming up."

"Well," she said, pretending to be picky, "I suppose that will have to do."

He was chuckling as he left the room. Kim began to undress. It was easy to strip out of her uniform—khakis and a polo shirt—but she hesitated with her underwear. She knew it was stupid. How many years had she been changing in a locker room? And what good was a massage if the work had to go through clothing? In fact, she'd been having sports massages for years when she wore absolutely nothing except the sheet. But suddenly the idea of a man's hands on her body had a whole new meaning.

She knew she was being ridiculous. True, David was her best friend, one who was suddenly way hotter and lust-inducing than ever before. But he was also a coworker giving a facial. In a business sense, he was as professional as they came. So with a bizarre sense of liberation—as if she were throwing off chains—she stripped out of her panties and bra. A moment later, she was wrapped in the spa towel and slipping underneath the blanket on the table.

"I'm ready," she called. Then she closed her eyes and prepared to be treated like a goddess.

Whatever David wanted to do to her—*for* her—she was ready.

Chapter Four

Kim tried to relax, but there was way too much David in the room. Even before he knocked and entered, she'd felt him like a physical caress. But now he walked in — all quiet, shirtless, and looking at her like he wanted to eat her. She felt herself flush and look away. What did she do when a guy looked at her like that? She was way too old to be confused by this, but she was.

She took a deep breath, feeling her nipples tighten, and tried to remind herself that they were just friends. Fortunately, David had shifted to the stool above her head. He was sitting down and her very first facial was about to begin.

"Just relax, Kim. I'm going to start with a hot towel." His voice was a low murmur, loud enough to hear, but deep enough to send a quiet thrill down her spine. Then he wrapped a moist, hot towel around her face. All of a sudden her breath was surrounded by sweet heat, her skin relaxed into the moisture, and the muscles between her eyebrows—the ones that were always pinched tight—just eased apart.

"Oh my God, that's awesome," she said.

She heard his chuckle. "I'll tell you a secret. Sometimes I heat up a towel, then wrap my head in it. I just stand here, all alone, with a towel on my face."

"Can I do it, too? Like right after staff meetings?"

"I'll join you. We'll make it a duo."

She smiled even though she didn't want to move a single muscle in her face. She could just picture them, sneaking into a spa room and wrapping themselves up like mummies.

But then the towel was cooling off, so he unwrapped it and began gently smoothing something onto her skin. The first thing she noticed was the scent. Raspberry and vanilla. The next was how perfect his caress was. Just hard enough to ease the tension in her face, but not so hard that she wanted to wince. She released a sigh of delight. It was stupid, really. This was turning her on. Her blood was simmering, her legs were getting restless, and deep in her belly was a warmth she knew could grow into a bonfire.

It was hormones, she told herself. Just chemical compounds zipping through her bloodstream and causing havoc. Nothing real. "What is this stuff?" she asked, just to distract herself.

He told her. She didn't even hear him. She was more interested in the cadence of his voice and the rumble of that male throat. She used to hear her father that way, back when he'd still been alive. His voice had come through the wall to the bedroom where she and her sister slept. It was a sound that meant security to her. A happiness that had disappeared the day he'd died.

Dave's fingers left her face to stroke up her neck. Whatever it was felt thick on her skin, but not unpleasant. And the way he eased her throat reminded her of something a nurse had done once when she'd had a really bad sore throat.

Childhood memories slipped through her mind. One flowed in, another flowed out. Nothing substantial and some not so pleasant, but then the ugly memories slipped away. The nicer ones lingered until she was floating in a sea of happy feelings. And then Dave's magic fingers went to the curve of her ears.

"You're not putting mud there, are you?"

He laughed, that low rumble that now vibrated delightfully down her spine. She would have to make sure she kept him laughing so she could feel it again. Then she realized that she was wet between her thighs. Wet and achy in a way she'd never been before. Good God, all he'd done was stroke her ears.

"Nope," he said. "This is just 'cause it feels good. You'd be surprised what kind of tension can be found in the ears. I know it doesn't make sense. No muscles here." He pinched the top of her ear and slowly massaged circles as he slid all the way around the lobe and down. "But I think we hear so much crap, the cartilage tightens up in response."

"Makes sense," she said.

"No, it doesn't. It makes no sense at all, but it still feels good."

She couldn't argue with that. Then when her ears felt like softened lumps of relaxed goo, he wet a towelette and began wiping off her face.

"What are you smiling at?" he asked.

"I was just thinking how manly your touch is."

There was a slight hitch in his movements. "Manly? This?"

She pouted in pretend insult. "If you can say my ears are stiff from the crap I hear, I can say that your strokes are very manly. Strong, assured, and very studly."

His movements resumed. "The client is always right. Therefore, I am a god among men."

"Well," she teased, "I wouldn't quite say *god*."

He chuckled, and again her spine tingled in response. "Just you wait. You'll be calling me a god before this night is over."

"Is that a promise?"

"You can take it to the bank."

"Good. 'Cause now you've said it, you're going to have to live up to it."

"I'm trembling in fear," he said, indicating he was anything but.

"I have very high standards for godliness, you know," she countered because she liked bantering with him. It was fun. It was flirty. And it relaxed her like nothing else could.

"Trust me, Kim. You won't be disappointed."

There was a gravelly sound to his voice, a thickness that hit her in a way she'd never experienced. It was almost primitive, and she was startled at how appealing that was. But then the thought fled as he wrapped another blessed, moist towel around her face.

She released a sigh of delight. "Okay, you're definitely climbing the steps to godhood."

His voice whispered through the towel to her ear. "Darlin', I'm just getting started."

And he was. Soon the towel was off and more stuff was going on. There was scented lavender, she thought. Another nice smell, but not her favorite raspberry. Then as she lay there with her face slathered, his fingers trailed into her hair. His touch started soothing, but before long, he was massaging her scalp and she was hard put not to moan.

"I could start listing the muscles of the scalp," he said as he worked, "but you'd be bored to tears. Let me just tell you what you need to know: you've got a headache. You probably *always* have a headache, but you're so used to it, you don't even notice."

She wanted to argue with him. She wanted to tell him that if she didn't notice the pain, then it wasn't important. But apparently it *was* important because the moment his fingers started easing the tension, everything in her world started to get better. Suddenly she didn't feel so beaten down. She breathed easier, and she even felt taller. Stupid when she was lying down, but what he did was like water to a dying plant. All of a sudden, she was beginning to perk up. And she never wanted it to stop.

"Do all your clients melt into a puddle on your table?"

"Only the best ones."

Then he started moving lower, slipping his hands beneath her and using her body weight to produce the pressure. He went from her scalp to the base of her skull, then to her neck and shoulders. Every push of his fingers, every deep circle had her opening up to him. Not just in body, but in mind. She began to trust him in a deeper way than ever before. Which was strange because over the past three years, he'd been an integral part of every day. He knew more about her than anyone. And yet, at this moment, he became more to her. He could probably ask her to give over state secrets and she'd whisper them without a second thought. And if he asked her anything more personal—like if she'd fantasized about the two of them together—then she'd tell him that too. Thank God he wasn't asking.

Then he went lower along her back. Down the spine, past the shoulder blades, until he hit her scar. Left side, the width of a blade as it slipped between two ribs.

Oh shit. That was a secret she hadn't shared with him. She didn't even like acknowledging it was there.

He was just kneading it, but she felt the hitch in his fingers as he hit the raised lump. And as he hitched, she tensed.

"Does it hurt?" he asked.

She swallowed, struggling with an unexpected surge of emotions. Fear, anxiety, embarrassment, and a host of other words flashed through her consciousness. In the end, she shook her head. "Not like you're thinking. Not like physical pain." It was the memories that cut.

He spread his fingers. He didn't leave the area, but he opened his hand to it like a bandage over a wound. And oddly, the heat of his palm felt really nice.

"Our tissues hold memories," he said. "I know it doesn't make sense, but I can already tell that this area is trapping a whole lot of crap. It doesn't have to be now, Kim, but you'll need to release this sometime."

She blinked, startled to feel the burn in her eyes as tears formed. So she made a joke to decrease her tension. "It's on my back, Dave. Out of sight, out of mind."

"But not out of body," he said gently.

"If it ain't broke, don't fix it. I function just fine—"

"Did you know you curl your left shoulder inward?"

She blinked, startled. "What? I do not!"

He shifted his right hand to her chest, directly over her

left shoulder. With a slight press, he proved to her exactly how wrong she was.

"There's always a little curl, but when you're feeling especially vulnerable, I see your shoulders go up and this one curl in. I never knew why until now. You're hunching away from this." He opened his hand even further as her scar settled deeply into his palm. "Whatever *this* is."

It was on the tip of her tongue to use the standard lie: a bike accident when she was a kid. No big deal. But she couldn't lie to him. Not David. So the words slipped out before she could second guess the decision.

"A knife," she whispered. "I was stabbed. When I was eleven."

"Eleven? Jesus." Then he paused. "Wait…"

He'd figured it out. He'd put the pieces together even though she never talked about it. But one Christmas party when she'd been sampling the eggnog, he'd asked about her family and she'd told him her father had died when she was eleven. Most people wouldn't remember little details like that, but David was different from anyone else she knew. He remembered. He seemed to remember *everything* about her.

"Yeah," she said, her voice thick and hoarse. "The night my dad died."

"I thought he had a heart attack."

"That's what I tell people," she said with a shrug, but the movement was especially awkward with his hands on her. He must have felt the tension in the movement. And oddly enough, just his quiet presence touching her seemed to drain away the worst of her anxiety. So as her fear left, it suddenly became easier to tell the whole truth. "But it was a heart attack from being stabbed in the chest."

"Oh my God."

She swallowed, the words flowing without her consciously willing them. Which was really odd, because just speaking aloud felt as if it were ripping through her throat. Still, she kept talking.

"Mom and my sister were out doing a Girl Scout thing. Gone all afternoon, but Dad had the day off. It was summer and the county fair was going on, so he took me." She blinked against the burn in her eyes.

"Is that why you hate cotton candy?"

Of course he would remember that. "Yeah. Just looking at it makes me sick."

"I take it you enjoyed the junk food at the fair."

She snorted. "Everything and anything he would buy me, but the cotton candy is what pushed me over the edge."

"You got sick?"

"Oh yeah. In a trash bin behind the pigs."

His hand was shifting now. The one on the scar was rolling in a small circle, around and around very slowly. It was nice what he did. A little painful, but it was a good kind of pain. As if something that was stuck was being slowly worked free. Meanwhile, her mouth just kept going.

"It was late anyway—after dark—but the hurling in the trash bin ended the day. He picked me up and carried me to the car. I still remember how that felt. He was bouncing me a bit as he carried me, and that made the nausea worse, but I never said a word. I was almost a teenager and not that small, but my dad was strong enough to carry me. And he hadn't done that for years. So I didn't say a word and…" Her throat closed down.

"And it was perfect. Your dad carrying you to the car

after a perfect day at the county fair. Of course you didn't stop him."

She nodded. No reason to belabor the story. "We were mugged. Two guys at first. Junkies with knives. Dad might have fought them off, but he was holding me."

"My kid in my arms? Hell, I'd have tried to hold off an army."

She nodded. "He did. Or at least he tried. At first he was just going to give them everything they wanted. Wallet, whatever. Just don't hurt his baby." Her voice cracked on that. Her dad had loved her. He'd died trying to protect her.

"It didn't work?"

"It did at first. But then a third guy showed up. He was jonesing hard. Dad didn't have enough cash—he'd spent it all on me at the fair—and they started to argue about it. Dad tried to get us away. They had his wallet, but one of them turned on him." She blinked as tears slipped down her cheeks. "On me."

"On you? You were only eleven."

"Guaranteed a virgin. I could be sold for a good price." Apparently, they'd stumbled on to the one junkie in Chicago who had a white slavery connection. Or maybe the bastard had just meant the local brothel. She didn't know, but she remembered how her father had suddenly gone ballistic.

"Oh my God, Kim."

"He fought like a demon, but there were three of them and I was screaming. He wanted me to run, but he was stabbed and I just waded in with only my fists. God, I was such an idiot. If I'd just run at the beginning like he'd said, then he could have run, too. I don't know."

"No," David said gently. "Then you'd just be torturing yourself for abandoning him to die. It was ugly no matter what you did."

She sighed. "Yeah, I know." And she did know that, in her head.

"But your heart holds on to the guilt, doesn't it? And your body too," he said, and she again realized that he was doing those slow circles along the scar. The opposite direction this time, and it felt really...good. "So how did you get the scar?"

"Knife. To shut me up. I was still screaming the whole time. Fortunately, there were people coming, so the bastards took off."

She felt his hand shake. She didn't know if it was a massage technique or if she'd given him the shudders. She shouldn't have told him this. It was too dark a story for most people to handle. Sure, they saw it on TV, but to know someone who... Well, she shouldn't have said anything.

She turned her face away, but he used his free hand to gently ease her back to look at him. And when she wouldn't, he stepped around the table, still keeping his hand beneath her, the one centered on her scar.

"That's the bravest thing I've ever heard."

She blinked. "Brave? I got my father killed."

"You were eleven. He was protecting you. That's a father's job. But that you tried to fight with your father—"

"I was just angry. And terrified."

"And very, very brave."

She blinked. More damn tears. He brushed them away, his stroke gentle. "I don't know why I'm crying," she said. "It was a long time ago."

"Like I said, tissues hold stuff. Scar tissue most of all."

"I'm not crying because you're massaging my scar."

"You're crying because you lost your dad. That's not something that goes away with time. It might ease a little, the ache might dull a bit, but it never goes away."

She swallowed. She couldn't speak past the lump in her throat. He didn't say anything, just continued to wipe away her tears. And as he did, she looked in his blue, blue eyes and let herself get lost.

Blue eyes. Gentle stroke. And the slow easing of pain.

"Do you charge extra for the psychotherapy?"

He smiled. "All part of the basic service." Then his expression sobered. "I think I understand now why you're obsessive about teaching that self-defense class. I'm so sorry, Kim."

"Thank you," she whispered, her mind caught up in releasing the horror of that awful day. Oddly, it didn't take as long as usual. With Dave touching her, everything in her seemed to ease.

Then he said something else, his voice so soft she had to strain to hear it. "I'm going to do something now, Kim. It's a little weird, so don't freak out. "

She frowned, then peered up at him. "Something?"

He nodded, his expression serious. "Something…well… something unprofessional."

Chapter Five

David held himself still. Not just his breath, but his entire life seemed suspended as he watched her think. They'd known each other for years, but this was the closest he'd ever gotten to her. He knew for damn sure no one else knew about what happened to her father.

Jesus, to watch your father die while protecting you? That had to be a mind-fuck of epic proportions. But here she was: strong, powerful, and so sexy it made his balls clench.

Did she trust him?

"What are you going to do?" Her voice was low and throaty.

He smiled. "I'm…I'm just going to talk to your scar. As I try to loosen up the tissues." Then he took a deep breath. "I know it sounds weird, but—"

She laughed, though the sound was stilted and rough. "Relax, Dave. I work in the fitness industry. You think I haven't heard my share of ultra-weirdness? Compared to the things I've heard, talking to your pain—or a scar—is practically established medical science."

He released a breath, knowing that he was one step closer to his ultimate goal. "But first," he said, moving to the top of the table bed, "let me get this off your face."

Given the time he'd taken massaging her head and neck, the mud on her face had stayed on much too long. But that was quickly remedied as he washed it off, did another hot towel treatment, and then finished up with astringent, then moisturizing lotion. He worked gently, already putting himself in the mindset of what he wanted to do to her back. And by the time he was done, she was as relaxed and receptive as she was going to get.

"Okay," he said, as he slid his hands down the outside of the covering sheet. "Do you think you could turn over for me?"

"Sure," she said, her voice low and a little dreamy.

Perfect.

He lifted the sheet, holding it up so that it blocked his view of her—damn it. But it also shielded his erection, so that evened it out. Besides, he was about to see much more of her than ever before, so he really didn't have grounds to complain.

She settled facedown and he draped the covering over her. Then he gently folded it away from her shoulders. Then another fold to reveal her back. Then one more time to just where the curve of her buttocks lifted.

Damn, she was beautiful. All that creamy golden skin. Her hair was coiled loosely to the side—lazy brown curls that were usually pulled back into a ponytail. But he'd taken the tie out for the head massage, so now her hair lay in swirls along her shoulder. Odd how sexy he found the sight of those soft curls beside the slope of her shoulder. It was as erotic a sight as the one that he'd exposed as he'd lowered the towel. Or maybe not, because everything about her back called to him: the clear cut of her shoulder blades and steady march of her spine. Her new curves made her soft, but he knew the muscles underneath and the solid strength of her. The dip in her waist was perfect, and he couldn't let himself look too long at the lift of her buttocks. Otherwise he was going to lose control completely.

So he took a breath and allowed himself to admire her for one more moment, then focused on the single jarring note on her body--the scar that ran for two inches along her left side. Focusing there, he touched it lightly and felt her skin ripple in anxiety. Then she abruptly pushed up on her forearms.

"Hell, what time is it?" she asked, looking around for the clock. "We've gone way beyond the scheduled time."

"No, we haven't," he lied as he gently pushed her back down. "Besides, I've got nothing at home for me tonight, re- member? And neither do you." He leaned down, allowing his breath to touch her neck where he wanted to put his lips. "We're doing this, so quit stalling. You either trust me or you don't."

It wasn't that black and white, and he knew it. But he also knew she never backed down from a challenge, even an implied one. "Of course I trust you," she answered, just as he knew she would. Then she fit actions to her words. She shivered and slowly eased her body down. "I'm just a little jumpy, okay?"

"I know," he said. "But I'd never hurt you." And then he

let himself do it. He let his lips brush the curve of her shoulder. The touch sent a bolt of *want* straight to his dick, but he blocked that from his brain. He didn't want to scare her. He had to go slow.

So he pulled back as if that had been an accident. Then he began to stroke her gently across her back. He did everything he could to relax her. Long, straight strokes; soft, feathery, gentle ones. Deep trigger points, and then the slow, mesmerizing circles that she'd responded so well to earlier. He didn't avoid the scar, but neither did he focus on it. He simply worked her back—and inched the sheet a little lower—as he talked.

The words were simple at first. "Look how beautiful you are. Every inch of you is perfection."

She snorted at that, but he ignored it beyond a quiet admonishment.

"This isn't going to work if you fight me, Kim. Just relax and let everything sink in."

She didn't answer except to give him a slow nod. He smiled and rewarded her with a single, deep trigger point press just above the scar. The muscles gave way—some—and he heard her moan softly in relief.

So he resumed his talk. He began with gratitude, thanking the skin for protecting Kim. He thanked the tissues beneath in detail, dredging up everything he knew about anatomy. Then he thanked the scar tissue for healing and protecting her. After that, he asked the tissues by name to release the pain. As he worked, he tried to mentally send the area peace and joy. He added *love* silently from his heart to hers.

And when he judged she was ready, he got more personal.

. . .

If anyone had told Kim she'd be lying facedown while a man talked to her scar, she would have laughed out loud. If someone had mentioned she'd be *mesmerized*, she would have written him or her off as a flake. But here she was, naked except for a sheet that didn't fully cover her bottom, while David made love to her scar.

That wasn't what he was doing, of course. Not really. But he was thanking it, and caressing it, and… Well, it felt like he was making love to it.

And it was *wonderful*.

She'd never felt so tenderly caressed, so sweetly worshipped. It was for her *scar*, damn it, and yet she felt what he did in every single cell of her body. Most especially the ones between her thighs.

God, she was wet for him. Her breasts were full, her body aching and hungry for his touch. Not on her back, but everywhere. And she wanted him hot and hard between her thighs too. The idea that he might pound into her was so bizarre. She never thought that way, but she was now. How awful that she was thinking sexually when her *friend* was doing something special right now. He was releasing the pain in her tissues, and he was doing it out of kindness. Not out of the need to be banging her from here to next Tuesday.

But oh, how she wanted him to. Her legs were spreading, even now. She'd die of mortification if he noticed. Thankfully, he was…

Oh my God! Was that his lips? Was he kissing her scar? She felt his mouth on her skin, the press of his lips, the stroke of his tongue. Long, wet strokes at first. Then tight swirls. His hands were framing the area, still stroking her, still keeping her a loose, receptive puddle of *yes!*

Then it was teeth. Light scrape, followed by a kiss, and then a gentle massage with his fingers. It was incredible—and it was all for her scar.

His words started sinking into her consciousness. They were murmured, but she heard them. Or maybe she imagined them. She didn't know, but her body responded as if he'd said those incredible words straight to her.

"You awe me. I watch you all the time, and I'm amazed by your strength. But sometimes you seem so alone. I just want to be there beside you, to help you however you need. To be the man you've always wanted in your life."

She gasped, her eyes rolling back in her head as his voice seemed to reverberate through her skin. Her belly tightened, her hands clenched the sheet. But she would do nothing to stop the flow of his kisses along her back or the words that meant so much to her.

"I want you, Kim. Hell, I love you. I always have."

That did it.

Oh God, her body arched off the bed, pleasure spiraling through her in waves of contractions. Holy shit—she'd just had an orgasm. That's what all the fuss was about, and it was *wonderful*. She was gasping, crying out in disorientation, in pleasure, in just plain...wow.

"Shhhh," he murmured. "Just enjoy it."

She couldn't catch her breath. The sensations were so amazing, and yet she was experiencing equal measures of humiliation. Had she just orgasmed from *words*?

"It's okay."

"No," she gasped, horrified even as the glow continued to suffuse her body. "It's not okay!" She tried to curl into herself. She tried to run away and hide. Somewhere like Tibet. But he didn't let her go. And her body wasn't yet under her control.

"Of course it is. Kim…Kim!" He held her arms still, half wrapping himself around her back to keep her down. Her knees were slightly bent and her arms were almost fully extended. In this position, the sheet had slipped down and now her bare ass was open to the air.

"Oh hell, David. I'm so sorry."

She felt his chuckle all the way through her body. And then when she stiffened in reaction, he quickly apologized. "No, no, I'm sorry. It's just that I gave you an orgasm. From kissing your back. Do you know what a dream come true that is for a guy?"

She took a breath, a flash of normalcy easing the panic inside her. This was Dave. If she could inappropriately orgasm in front of anyone, it would be him. Right?

"Made your day, didn't it?" she quipped.

"Made my decade. Hell, it made my life."

She settled back down onto the bed. In truth, she had no choice. Her body was still languid after that eruption of pleasure. Meanwhile, he eased off his grip on her shoulders. But as he moved, he slid one of his hands down her arm.

"Look, as long as we're being inappropriate, let me show you something."

He worked his way down to her hand and then slowly brought her to his groin. Holy hell, he was huge. And hot. And really, really hard for her.

"You're not the only one turned on here. You can't

imagine the fantasies that are rolling through my brain." Then he released an anxious laugh. "I suppose I shouldn't say that."

He let go of her hand, but she didn't let go of him. She'd never explored a man before. Sure, she had seen a penis before. She'd touched her boyfriends, even gone down on a couple. But she'd only done so because the guys had wanted her to, and she'd thought she was missing something by not doing it. But in the end, it had never been fun for her. And she'd certainly never orgasmed from it.

Good lord, how much of a normal life had she lost when she started training? And she'd never even realized the lack because she'd stopped developing or rather, she'd slowed the process down to a crawl. But now her hormones were back with a vengeance and she wanted to find out all those things she'd missed in her life.

"Uh, Kim? You can let go anytime now."

"Hmmm," she purred, her hand tightening against him. His sweatpants were really thin. Old soft cotton that really wasn't much of a barrier. And if she wasn't mistaken, there was some moisture wetting the fabric. "No, I don't think I want to let go. Not yet, at least."

She heard him swallow. She actually heard it.

And right then she had a decision to make. He wanted her. She was so keyed up, she'd just had her very first orgasm. How much further did she want to take this? How much more did she want to experience?

Everything.

The answer came between one breath and the next. She was twenty-four years old. Her athletic career was over. Why not explore some of the things she'd been denied so long? And why not do it with a friend like David? Someone she trusted. Someone who had already just seen her be inappropriate. Why not be very unprofessional together?

Easy decision. Especially given the pornographic thoughts she'd been having about him lately. And that incredible kiss they'd shared. Suddenly the danger to their friendship didn't seem like such a big risk anymore. So she took a deep breath and went for it.

She rolled on her side just enough to flash him her breasts. And to watch his face as she did it. Yup, another swallow. And his gaze had zeroed in right on her tight nipples.

"Tell me one."

"One?"

"Fantasy. You said you had fantasies rolling through your brain right now."

"Oh," he said. "That."

She gave him her most flirtatious expression. She wasn't good at it, but it seemed to do the trick.

"You," he said in a raspy breath. "Just like that. Or maybe up a bit on all fours." Then he flushed as if he couldn't believe he'd just said that aloud. She, however, was thrilled to death.

"Behind me?" Yes, she wanted to try that. "You clean?"

He nodded, the motion jerky. "Very. Plus, I have condoms."

Her eyebrows rose. "Seriously?"

His hand twitched to the side table. After all, she still had him gripped in her hand and now she was rolling her thumb along the ridge of his head. "Sometimes couples rent the rooms. You know that."

"Ah yes. I'd forgotten." Then with a quick flick of her wrist, she tugged his sweats out and down. She didn't get far. He was that huge. But she cleared his head and was now able to touch him for real.

"Kim…"

She grinned, her attention riveted to his glistening tip. "Give me a moment. I'm exploring."

He groaned and she laughed. But all too soon, she wanted to know more. Experience more. She glanced up at his half-closed eyes. "What should I do? Just get up on all fours?"He jerked, but he didn't move much farther. "Are you sure? A moment ago, you were apologizing."

"A moment ago, I didn't realize you wanted it, too." She frowned. "You do, don't you?"

"More than I want my next breath."

"Well, lucky you. You get to do both—me and breathe—all at once."

He didn't waste any time. His pants hit the floor at the same time as he pulled open the drawer. Then he was ripping open the foil package with his teeth. Damn, how could teeth look so sexy? But this did. His even teeth, the intense burn to his blue eyes, and the way his whole body was hard for her. Taut and hard.

She couldn't wait.

He struggled a bit to roll on the condom. That actually endeared him to her even more. Except that the way he crossed to the back of the table was full of confidence and the powerful play of muscles.

He put his hand on her leg and she felt his fingers tighten. "I gotta tell you," he said, his voice ragged. "I'm on the edge here. I don't want to hurt you."

A thrill went through her body at that. Meanwhile, his hands were on her hips, helping her shed the spa wrap as she turned to get up on her hands and knees. Within a moment, she was naked and exposed, but she didn't care. She was with David and suddenly, one of her fantasies was coming true.

She was just getting used to the idea when he tugged her toward him. She flew backward in shock, but he had her safe. He caught her and helped her slide down. Her feet hit the floor, his hands caressing her as her upper body stretched out on the table. Not really all fours, but more bent over as he snuggled tight behind her, his hot cock pressed against her backside. Unfortunately, her position wasn't quite at the right height for him to slip between her thighs, but—go figure—there were electric pedals to raise and lower the table bed. He didn't even have to move to get her where he wanted.

A second later and she felt him there—thick and insistent. Was she really doing this? Then *slam*.

She cried out. The pain was sharp and so unexpected. Her virginity gone in a pierce of pain.

He froze, his breath hot on her back. "Oh shit. Oh God. You're a virgin. Kim, you said you've had sex. You told me that."

"Oral sex," she said, her words coming out in a stuttered pant. He was so huge! But she was getting used to it. The feel of stretching open to him, of her legs and her whole body surrounding him, oh God, it was amazing.

"Kim… Is it bad?"

She shook her head. "No," she whispered. Now it was starting to feel good.

He pressed gentle kisses onto her back, and she hummed in appreciation. Meanwhile, her breath was evening out, her body growing languid. "So is that it?" she teased, already knowing the answer. "Or is there more?"

She felt his hands tighten slightly on her hips. "I don't want to make it worse."

She giggled and was pleased to hear him groan. "There is no bad here. Now show me what I want to learn."

He paused for a moment, clearly processing her words. And then she did something she'd heard about but never tried. After all, she'd taught all those classes that used Kegel exercises. She might as well see if they worked.

So she squeezed her internal muscles, doing something she'd heard about from another instructor. One long squeeze, followed up by a couple shorter bursts.

"Holy shit!" he gasped. Then he stopped speaking because he was starting to move. She held her breath, worried despite what she'd just said. Would it hurt? Was he going to get too rough?

No and no. The way he slid out left her feeling empty. But then he pushed back in, slow at first and then the next time harder. Faster. She heard his breath grow shorter, and his body thicker somehow. Wonderfully big as he pounded into her and she was crying out at every steady, fabulous slam.

Another orgasm hit, rolling through her spine, making him cry out. He slammed into her again, his hands gripping her tight, and she felt him explode. God, it was great to feel so powerful a man bursting inside her. He was spasming, his thighs pinning her against the table as he released over and over. Her own contractions were extending his. They were feeding each other, and the pleasure was indescribable.

It was the best damn facial/massage she'd ever had.

Good thing she was lying on the table, because no part

of her body had any strength. Her upper body was draped across the bed and her lower half was still supported by him.

Had he actually lifted her off the ground with his thrusts? God, how awesome was that?

He slowly leaned down, pressing kisses into her back. They weren't coordinated strokes like before. Just presses against her skin as he slowly collapsed on top of her.

"I'm going to move in a second," he murmured. "Tell me if I get too heavy."

"What heavy?" she said, obviously not very coherent yet. "I'm still floating."

"I'm still in heaven."

She smiled. "Good place to be, considering."

"Considering?"

She twisted slightly. "Considering you're a god."

She felt him still, then abruptly smile. His chuckle rolled straight through her from where he was still embedded deep, all the way up her spine. It felt good, and she started to laugh, too. Then he pressed a kiss to her shoulder.

"I'm inspired," he said.

"I think I'm still coming," she said as another small ripple rolled through her.

He groaned in pleasure, his organ kicking inside her. "Can we do this again, please? Sometime really damn soon?"

"Yes," she said without thought, though inside she felt herself clench. What was she getting into here? What about all her fears about their friendship? What if—

"You're starting to tighten up."

"Well, you are getting a little heavy," she lied.

He was immediately contrite as he straightened. A moment later, he was pulling out of her and cleaning up. And then he was back next to her, gently urging her back onto the table.

"What are you doing?"

He smiled at her, but his expression seemed tighter than before. "The least I can do is clean you up."

"Oh! Oh no!" she cried. The idea was vaguely horrifying. "I can do that."

"Of course you can, but Kim… I promised you a full body massage."

She snorted. "I think I've gotten my money's worth."

He touched her face, and her traitorous body just melted into his palm. It didn't matter that she was feeling awkward. That her biggest fear of things going weird between them was starting to materialize. All that seemed to matter to her right then was feeling him touch her again. All over.

"I need to make this right between us," he said. "I don't want it to be weird."

"It's not weird," And it wasn't. Well, not completely.

He kissed her. Deep and full and once she got over the shock of it, she opened for him.

She loved the thrust of his tongue, the possession of his mouth, even the way he dominated her enough that her head fell back onto the bed. She was lying half-twisted, all the way naked, and suddenly thinking became way overrated.

So when he ended the kiss, pulling back in a slow separation while they both took deep breaths, she had the strength to put her hand on his rippling pecs.

"You know what?" she said with a smile. "I think I want that massage. And I think I want you to do it naked."

His mouth parted on a gasp, but his eyes had suddenly gone dark as his nostrils flared. And if she didn't believe what she saw there, he was wrapped around her enough that she felt his cock jerk against her hip. He wanted her. Better yet, within about five minutes, he'd be ready for her again.

"Naked, huh?" he said with a sexy drawl. "Guess that means you're going for the full treatment."

"You better believe it."

He frowned a moment. "But you were a virgin, Kim. That means—"

"And a full-grown adult." She gave him a small smile. She'd spent nearly a quarter century ignoring this part of her life in favor of training, of school, of *work*. It was about damn time she caught up in other areas of life. The fact that she was doing it with her best friend only made it more special. "I chose you, David. Let me learn about this with you."

His expression went almost radiant. He looked stunned and awed and so damn happy. Then he swallowed. "You might be sore."

She frowned. "Isn't there a way to prevent that?"

He laughed, the sound easier than she'd ever heard from him. "Um, yeah. Some ways. And I suppose, if you're hurting tomorrow, I could always give you another massage."

She grinned. "I like the sound of that." Then she curled her finger, urging him to step closer to her along the bed. It took him a moment, but he complied until he was right where she wanted him: his cock next to her face. This was something she knew how to do, and she was eager to try it when her hormones were fully engaged.

"Here," she said with a grin. "Let me help with that." Then she leaned down and engulfed him.

Chapter Six

David nearly fell down, but that would have ended the glorious sensations rolling through his dick and from there to the rest of his body.

She was sucking on him! Good God, he never thought he'd come to this moment. Certainly not today. Possibly not ever. But here she was—Kim, the woman he'd been lusting after since the day he'd met her, sucking on him.

Unable to support himself, he leaned forward, bracing his arms on the table. This close, he could smell her scent. The lavender he'd used on her face, the raspberry he'd mixed into the oil, and her. Sweet, musky, glorious Kim. He licked his lips and thought about when he'd return the favor to her. But first…

Holy God. He shivered as her tongue ran the length of him. Then she abruptly straightened up. "Hold on a sec," she said, her voice all husky. "Don't move."

As if he could…

She straightened and spun around, going quickly to the sink area. It took her less than a minute. After all, she knew these rooms almost as well as he did. She grabbed a paper cup, then popped open the tiny refrigerator right below. A second later, she had the freezer part open and was slapping out some ice cubes.

"Kim?"

"Just a moment." She looked over her shoulder. "Spend the time looking at my ass." She wiggled for emphasis. She didn't need to; he'd been watching the sexy flex of her butt from the moment it came into view.

"Way ahead of you there. And if you don't hurry up, I'm going to lose control and pin you against that counter over there."

She laughed, which did all sorts of fun things to her back and butt. "Been there, done that. Besides, this one's for you."

Then she slid around the table and knelt before him, gently twisting his hips as she moved.

Lord, she was on her knees in front of him. He was going to come just from the sight. "You don't have to do this."

"Shut up, will you? I haven't been a total nun these years. And, well, I'm experimenting here."

She was smiling as she looked at him, all thick and aimed straight at her. She reached up and stroked him. A soft caress, a firmer grip. Her other hand joined in the play, slipping down to cup his sack, and he nearly collapsed from the pleasure of it.

"Kim—"

"Shhh," she said. Then she leaned over and popped an ice cube in her mouth. Before he could really process what she was doing, she engulfed him again. Her whole mouth—

his whole dick.

The cold shock of the ice hit him like a ton of bricks. Combined with the scorching heat of her mouth and really talented tongue, he nearly buckled. Or maybe not, because all of a sudden, biology took over. He was thrusting into her, harder and harder. He tried to be gentle, but she just kept teasing him. Ice cold, curling heat, then suction. Sweet Jesus, she was doing it all. And *taking* it all.

His hands slipped to her shoulders, gripping her hard. "Kim! I'm—I'm—"

She squeezed his sack, and he lost it. All. Right into her. And she swallowed. Every last drop.

It took him a moment to recover. Hell, it took him long eons to recover, but as he was regaining his strength, as his muscles stopped trembling and his mind began to clear, one thought lifted above the rest to burn into his consciousness. Or perhaps he focused on that one glorious thought rather than allow his mind to dwell on the dangers ahead. The fact that he still had to confess his theft to her or that she might regret losing her virginity in a tiny spa room. Right now, he was thinking about her and how he could give her more pleasure. It took him a minute to get the strength to act. But when he did, it was as though he had superpowers. She inspired him that much. Leaning down, he lifted her up. And up. Until he could set her gently on the bed.

"David?"

He grinned. "Your turn."

Then he flipped her legs over his shoulders and began to feast.

• • •

Kim had never thought she'd enjoy oral sex. Sure, she'd wanted to taste David. And really enjoyed the salty, sweet heat that was him. But to have a man lick her there? The idea was… The thought… Her mind stuttered out. David was licking her as if he knew exactly what he was doing.

It wasn't about just bringing her to orgasm. No, he acted like he enjoyed what he was doing and had all the time in the world to study her responses. Time after time, he took her to near orgasm, only to hold back. To knead her spread thighs, to wiggle his fingers inside her without ever pushing her over the edge. And then when she was mad with frenzy, writhing beneath him on the table bed, he sat back and just grinned. Grinned at her, the wretch! As if he was having the time of his life.

She couldn't stand much more. She tightened her legs, trying to pull him right back to where he'd been. No go. He was much too strong. Then she reached forward. She was going to haul him forward by his ears, but he caught her wrists.

"Damn it, David! You will finish what you started!"

"Or what?"

She gasped. She was cooling off and she did *not* like that. "Or…or I'll never get another facial again!"

He burst out laughing—a sensation that was both wonderful and *not enough*. "We can't have that, can we?" he said. Then he released her wrists. She fell backward because finally, *finally!* she'd get what she wanted. Except he didn't go back down on her.

"David?"

"I like to watch," he said. Then he slid his fingers inside her. Two or three, she couldn't be sure. Not with the way they were wiggling, the thick stretch of it all. But she was so slick, it was hard to tell what was what when it was all awesome and still *not enough!*

"David!"

"Patience is a virtue."

"I'm not virtuous!"

"Yeah, you are. And you're beautiful and amazing and—"

"David!"

He stroked her clit. A full press, a tight circle, and then a pinch. It was the pinch that sent her over the edge.

"—awesome," he said.

She barely heard him over her scream. Especially since he didn't stop. He kept pinching even as she bucked on the table. And when he couldn't hold on any longer, he pinned her thighs down with his arms and went back to eating her.

Holy shit, her mind went white.

. . .

She came back to herself on the table. He was cleaning her up—again. And this time she was much too boneless to be embarrassed.

"This is the best spa ever!" she murmured. "I'm going to recommend it to all my friends."

He chuckled but didn't speak. And as he worked, she marveled at how gentle his hands were. Every stroke, every smooth glide was done with a kind of tenderness that couldn't be faked. And yet even as she knew the feelings were genuine, she began to question them.

No man could possibly be this perfect. Selfless during sex, understanding of her pain, even healing with his every caress. It wasn't possible. This wasn't real though she wanted it to be. She wanted to believe the illusion with every fiber of her being.

"I'm losing you. You're pulling away."

"What?" She pushed up on her elbow to look at him. She even let the sheet fall off her breasts just to prove to him that she hadn't withdrawn.

He looked at her, his gaze dropping immediately to her chest. His expression softened and his hand reached out. He stroked her gently, reverently, and she shivered in response, her nipples tightening to hard points.

But then he let his hand drop back to his side. "I don't mean sexually, Kim." He pulled the sheet back up to cover her torso. "I think you and I will always fit this way."

"Uh, yeah. I think we've established chemistry."

"I'm talking about here." He tapped her forehead. "And here." He pressed his palm flat to the center of his chest.

"You're asking for my heart and mind? Seriously?" She flopped backward to cover her unease. This was all so new. She wasn't a pro athlete anymore. She was just learning who she was outside of that identity. And now she'd just lost her virginity. Awesome experience, to be sure, but that wasn't the same thing as stepping into a relationship. So she shot him a teasing look. "Are you sure you're not gay? I mean when a guy talks about…" She couldn't even say the word *love*. And since *he* hadn't, she sure as hell wasn't going to. "About…"

"Feelings?"

"Yeah. Feelings. What guy brings those up first?"

"One who's lonely and has been waiting an awful long time for a friend to notice him."

She swallowed. This was getting pretty deep really fast.

"Dave…" Lord, she so didn't want to say this. "This has been a ton of fun."

"But we're friends, and you don't want to screw that up with a relationship."

He took the words right out of her mouth and, damn it, she wanted to bite him for doing that. She ought to be grateful. He was making it easy on her. He understood exactly what she was thinking, exactly where her head was. And yet she couldn't deny the feelings of betrayal here. He was obviously hurt. He clearly wanted more from her, when all she'd come in to have was a facial and a massage…

"Don't make this my fault," she said, her anger rising to cover how hurt she felt. Which made no sense at all.

"I'm not," he said, though from his tone, he was struggling to say those words. "I'm just disappointed."

"Oh my God, you *are* a girl!"

It was the wrong thing to say. She'd been turning away when suddenly he was there. Not just in her face, but towering over her. In the blink of an eye, he'd leaped to the side of the table and was putting his face straight up to hers.

"Do not trivialize this!"

She blinked, reaching for bravado to cover her shock. Because, damn, she'd never seen him looking so fierce. Hell, a second ago, she wouldn't have thought him capable of it. "Defensive much?" she tried to joke.

His nostrils flared, his eyes narrowed, and swear to God, she almost whimpered. Not because he'd physically hurt her. Hell, no. Not David. But she worried about what he was going to do to her emotionally. She was staring into the face of a man who was going to tear down her emotional walls. And that scared the shit out of her.

"I can be the *man* you want. I'm damn sure I'm the man you *need*."

She lifted her chin. Thank God for bravado or she'd be completely defenseless. "That's quite a tall order, *man*. I don't even know what I need. What makes you think you do?"

"I've been watching you from the very first day we met. And I've been paying attention."

That was both terrifying and incredibly flattering all at the same time. But she was deep in defense, so she simply raised her eyebrows at him. "Stalker?"

He shrugged, not denying it. "The line between love and obsession is such a fine one."

Oh hell, she'd hurt him. And hurt him badly from the mocking tone of his voice. He only went there when something — someone — really upset him. She swallowed, scrambling for some way to backtrack with him. And right here was what she'd most feared. Their friendship was suddenly changing. God, what was she going to do? She couldn't lose him!

"Look, Dave," she said, striving for a reasonable tone, "I've obviously crossed some sort of line here. I'm not sure what to do. I…uh…I don't want to lose…" She swallowed. The sex. The friendship. *Him*. All of those words flitted through her brain but none of them really fit. "I don't want to lose the good things we have."

"And what would those be? Tell me exactly."

She looked away. His eyes were too intense. His words and his needs were flaying her alive, and she just wasn't prepared for this. So she turned her face away and tried to hold back the tears.

"Don't you get it?" she said. "You're asking for more

than I can handle right now." She gathered her courage and turned back to face him. "You just stripped me naked and gave me the best sex I've ever had."

"The only sex," he repeated. Then he flushed and she heard him mutter a curse. "You're overwhelmed."

"No." *Yes.* "Look, I really just wanted…"

"A good time? A facial and a massage?" He made it sound as if she'd wanted something cheap and dirty.

"That's not fair!" she cried. "Damn it, I need a friend. And yeah, what we just did was amazing, but if the cost for tonight is our friendship…" She closed her eyes on a frustrated moan. God, she didn't even want to imagine that, let alone voice it out loud. "Please don't do that to me. Don't—"

He kissed her. Light, sweet, like a brush against her lips, but she opened to him. His tongue slipped inside on a teasing caress. It was everything gentle that was David, and she clung to it as she would a lifeline.

And then it was done. He pulled back, held a long moment, just looking at her. "We've got to talk. Maybe not right now, but…there are things I've got to tell you."

Holy shit, that sounded serious. "Dave—"

"I don't want you to pull away now because of this. Because there's more. More that we have to discuss."

What more could there be? He was already talking about feelings when she'd barely sorted out that sex with him was fabulous.

She lifted her head slightly, until they were separated by less than an inch. "You are one intense guy after sex, you know that?"

"That's because I've been waiting to talk to you." He flushed, and his expression grew apologetic. "I know I'm pushing. I know this is too fast for you. Hell, it's incredibly intense for me too, but…" His words cut off. And then before she could ask, he leaned down. He pressed another slow, sweet kiss to her lips. Then he abruptly stepped back. By the time she'd focused her eyes, he was standing there still gloriously naked and—*oh my*—thickly aroused, but his eyes were kind.

"You'll never lose that, Kim. Ever."

She blinked. What did that mean? Exactly? "So…we're good?"

"Sure," he said, his tone light. Then he turned away, pulling on his pants with quick, efficient movements. He was acting casual, as if the last five minutes hadn't happened. As if he hadn't shown her how deeply—how thoroughly—he wanted her. He wanted to possess every inch, every cell, every breath.

That's what he wanted. And she wanted to run screaming from the very idea.

"I'm just not ready for more," she said to his back. "I can't give you that much. Not yet."

He turned to face her. "Do you know what love is? It's making yourself vulnerable to someone else. About giving your everything—heart, mind, soul—over into his care. Because you trust him. And because he—because *I*—would never hurt you. I want only the best for you, and I'm so completely and deeply vulnerable to you, too." He abruptly ran a hand through his hair. "I don't want to lose you either."

She shook her head. "That's getting lost. Totally and completely lost in someone else. I won't do that. I need to be me."

"I love who you are. Why would I change you?"

She flinched. He'd used that damn word again. Well, it was time to rip off the bandage. It was time to give him the hard, cruel truth.

"But I don't love you, David. Not that way."

He didn't even flinch. He just nodded. "I know."

She frowned. "Then... Then why?"

"Why the sex? Why the best damn facial of my life? Are you kidding?" He leaned back on his heels. She saw the effort that it cost him, but suddenly he was all joking laughter as he gripped his very impressive package. "I am a guy, after all."

She snorted. And when he camped up his macho pose even more—flexing his pecs then curling his biceps—she just let go and started laughing.

Thank God! Thank God they were back on their friendship basis. Maybe this could work out. Maybe they could have a night like tonight without screwing up the rest of her life. Maybe.

She certainly prayed it was true.

She swung her feet around, sitting gingerly on the side of the table with the sheet still wrapped around her body. "David?"

He focused on her immediately. He lost the comic pose and just looked at her. And he was just David to her. Beautiful blue eyes, light-brown curly hair, lean body, and an open heart. Talk about vulnerable. He risked too much of himself, and on the wrong people.

God, she would kill anyone who hurt him. And she'd rip out her own tongue before she did anything to change him. If only she knew how to keep things right between them.

"Dave..."

He pressed his finger to her lips. "I know. But don't think I'm done with you yet."

A shiver ran down her spine. A nice shiver, filled with excitement and wonder and a good deal of sexual attraction. "Uh...what?"

He shook his head. "You were right. I moved too fast, spoke too soon."

"It's okay—"

"Damn right it's okay. *We're* okay, Kim. But there's going to be more nights like this. I don't know when exactly, but I'm going to show you that I know what you need. And I can provide it." He paused a moment, looking uncertain. "And then there's going to be the time when I have to be completely vulnerable to you. When I have to tell you everything, too."

Hadn't he already done that? Like when he started using the L-word? She touched his wrist, gently pulling his hand away from her face. She was both excited and terrified by what he said, and so she had to put the brakes on. She didn't like being on uncertain ground.

"I hate surprises. You should know that about me."

"I do. It's because you're kind of a control freak."

"I am not!"

"That's not what your staff says."

She snorted, but it was filled with humor. This was familiar ground between them. She wasn't really a control freak, but she was a stricter supervisor than he was. And that difference had given rise to this banter. Which meant it was time for her response. She spread her arms and shrugged. "I am who I am."

He smiled at her then, looking just like the easygoing

guy she'd known for years. "About that other thing…" he began, but she held up her hand.

"God, enough already. I'm done for tonight."

He nodded. "I know. But when you're ready, just ask me for the serious talk."

"Well, that will be never." She touched his arm, feeling his warmth, but also how the muscles tensed beneath her. "We're okay, right?" He'd already said they were, but she needed to hear it again.

"Always."

She waited a moment, needing to absorb that word into her bones. They were back where they'd started: as friends. But, of course, now there was some extra spice to that word. It wasn't just friends with benefits, it was friends with surprises. Friends with excitement. Friends with…

David.

"Come on," he said. "Get dressed. I'll walk you to your car."

"You don't have to walk me—"

"Just shut up. I know you're all macha and stuff, but let me be gallant here."

She grinned. "Okay, Sir Gallant, I will allow you to walk me to my car."

So she did. And he did. And all the while, she was wondering exactly what *they* would do in the very near future.

Chapter Seven

Kim's surprise came three days later, and it was anything but fun. She was signing on to the company accounting system. She was behind on the receipts and needed to get them done before tomorrow's staff meeting. But she never got that far.

It was a simple message, a computer window that welcomed her into the system and listed the last time she'd logged in: 9:37 p.m. on the night Frank Johnson had shoved her against the filing cabinet. She remembered it clearly, just as she knew she hadn't been in the system at all that day. And she certainly hadn't been working while the jerk was accosting her.

She rapidly thought back, her mind replaying that day in detail. Maybe she'd forgotten something. Maybe there was another explanation. But the more she thought about it, the more she knew she was right. David had been in her office that night with his lame excuse of falling asleep on her floor.

But he hadn't been sleeping, had he? No, it very much

looked as though he had been getting illegal access to their accounting software. But just to be sure, she called in tech support. Then she paced her office, thinking awful things, while she waited for them to figure out exactly what had happened.

Was it possible? Had David been stealing from her company? David, the man who had been her best friend for three years, who had given her her first orgasm—first of several orgasms—not three days before. Was it all a lie? Had it been a cover for…what? Theft? Embezzlement? God, the possibilities twisted in her mind, getting worse with every minute.

An hour later, there was no question. The computer geek sitting at her desk walked her through what he'd discovered. At 9:37 someone had logged in to her computer as her. Two minutes later, accounting books going back three years had been e-mailed to an address: davidpepke@pampermespa.com.

The betrayal was so deep and so painful that she nearly cried out. She did bite her cheek until she tasted blood. Then she thanked the man and changed all her passwords, before stomping down the connecting passages and straight into David's office.

He was working at his computer, his expression drawn as he tapped at the keys. Even as furious as she was, part of her still noted the chiseled cut to his jaw and the broad width to his shoulders. He was handsome, and even knowing that he'd used her to get access to the business accounts, she couldn't stop the pang of longing. Maybe there was another explanation. Maybe…

"Kim! What are you—"

"Did you do it? Did you hack my computer and e-mail our books to yourself?"

He didn't answer, but then again he didn't need to. At her words, the color drained from his face. His mouth dropped open, but no words came out.

"Oh God," she breathed. "You did."

He swallowed and straightened his shoulders. "I did, but you have to let me explain."

"Explain?" She all but screamed the word. "How can you explain that? Hacking? Corporate theft? Oh hell, I need to call John." She'd been so upset, she hadn't even thought about what she'd tell the fitness center's owner.

David was out of his seat before she did more than turn around. "Please, just…give me a chance to explain. Then afterward, you can call security or the cops or whomever you want."

She shook her head, not rejecting him, but because she didn't want to believe any of it. She didn't want to think that her best friend could have been lying to her all this time. "John will get you fired. Oh God, you could go to jail!"

He squeezed her arms, the gesture tender even though there was panic in his eyes. "Please, you've got to listen to me."

"How long? How long have you been lying to me?" She swallowed, thinking about what they'd done just a few nights ago. About their whole relationship over the last three years. Had he been using her this whole time? For what? To get access to the books? That made no sense.

"Not long, I swear."

"But at least since that night. Since before…" Before they'd done such amazing things together not twenty feet from where they were standing right now. She bit her lip, all but sobbing in her horror. "It was a lie…"

"The hell it was!" Then David cursed, the word as blisteringly loud as it was graphic. Then he visibly pulled himself together. "You have to come with me now. I have to show you something."

Kim shook her head, every horrible cop show she'd ever seen leaping to the forefront of her brain. Never go off alone with the desperate thief. Just call the cops and don't make yourself vulnerable. Anything else got you dead.

Dead? What was she thinking? This was David! But—

"Jesus, I'm not going to hurt you. I just want to explain." He gestured impatiently outside his office door. "Someplace else. Where we can't be overheard."

She shook her head, her mind and her heart at war. Nothing made sense. "I need to think."

"Here," he said hastily scribbling an address down on a pad of paper. Then he ripped off the page and handed it to her. "Go to this address. Drive in your own car. I'll meet you."

"What is this place?"

"It's our corporate offices for Pamper Me Spa. Everything you need to see is there. Please, Kim, trust me just this much. If I've ever meant anything to you, just…trust me this little bit."

What could she say to that? It might be stupid, but damn it, they were friends. More than that, they were lovers now and she just couldn't accept that he meant her harm.

"Remember what I said to you the other night—"

"We said a lot of things," she snapped.

"But I said there was something serious we needed to talk about. This is it. This is what I need to show you. I just…"

He sighed. "I was just looking for a better time."

"A better time," she echoed lamely. Like when she wasn't reeling from her first real sexual experience? "It's been three days."

"I know," he said, rubbing his hand over his face. "But we've both been so busy and you canceled yesterday when we were going to have lunch together."

Oh yeah. She had canceled. But—

"You can't trust me this little bit?" he asked. He didn't sound angry so much as resigned. And hurt.

She closed her eyes while her brain told her she was the biggest fool on the planet. She ignored it. "Okay," she finally said. "I'll go, but you better have a damn good explanation."

He exhaled in relief. "It's an explanation, at least. You're going to have to tell me if it's good enough."

• • •

They drove separately to the spa corporate offices. Kim spent the entire drive with her cell phone in hand, wondering if she should call John. Well, of course she should. It was his company and his accounting software that had been compromised. She had to tell him. But she could delay in the name of investigating. And that's what she was doing, right? Investigating exactly what had happened.

It was a gray line, but one she was embracing. She just couldn't believe that David had betrayed her like that. Corporate theft? What the hell? David was as devious as mashed potatoes. So she was going to let him explain before… Well, before she did something she'd regret.

She pulled into a parking space right beside David. Then,

when he got out of his car, he gestured her to an innocuous glass door with the Pamper Me Spa logo on the front. She went with him, stunned when the bland exterior turned into a tasteful, lush, *expensive* interior. She looked around. She'd known the chain was doing well, but by the looks of this, it was doing *very well.*

Then she got her second shock of the day as a tall, older man stepped out and greeted David with a hearty handshake. "David, I got your message."

"Hi, Uncle Carl. Thanks for meeting us."

Uncle? Kim did a double take, her eyes picking out the family similarities between the two men. Both had light-brown hair, though Carl's was a whole lot thinner than David's. Both had the same general build and those warm blue eyes. Eyes that were right now looking at her.

"This her?" Carl asked.

"Yes. Kim, this is Carl Pepke, CEO of Pamper Me Spa. Uncle Carl, this is Kim Castillo, manager of John's Fitness."

"Pleased to meet you," she said warily. "Look, I don't know what David has told you, but—"

"Let's go into David's office, shall we?"

Kim had taken a step before she pulled up short. "David's office?" She turned to her friend. She'd thought he was simply a manager at the franchise next to John's Fitness. Apparently, he was a lot more than that if he had an office here at corporate HQ.

His uncle's next words confirmed it. "Dave's part owner of the entire company. If it weren't for him, we'd still be just a small-time outfit of one little spa."

"Hardly—" David said, but his uncle kept going.

"Because of his work, we've grown into five high-end

spas. I just can't get him to relocate here. Something about the location next to John's Fitness has him locked down tight over there."

David didn't say anything, but something about his steady gaze on her made her guess at the reason. He'd stayed right where he was so he could be near her.

She swallowed, reeling from this new information. "But what does that have to do with my computer?" she asked.

David unlocked his office door and ushered her inside. His uncle followed but didn't sit. Instead, he handed her a huge file folder. She looked down, flipping it open and reading the top page. *Offer Memorandum for John's Fitness.* She swallowed and looked up. "You're trying to buy the club?"

David's uncle answered. "We are, but something's off with the numbers. Flip to the next document. That's what John claims it's worth."

Kim looked down, scanning the neat columns. She wasn't a CPA, but she had enough accounting knowledge to understand that something was very wrong with the numbers. The club wasn't pulling in that kind of income. Not by a long shot.

Then David lifted a page off his desk and passed it to her. "This is a list of the repairs John claims he's made to the building."

It took Kim less than a second to react to that. "But it's bullshit! Yeah, we worked on the air conditioner last summer, but we didn't replace it. Same with the Jacuzzi in the women's locker room. The interior painting was done three years ago, not two and…" Her voice trailed away as she started to understand what was going on. "John's been lying to you, trying to inflate the price with false documents."

"But I couldn't prove it without access to the real accounting books," Dave said, his expression grave.

"For the record," inserted his uncle, "it was my idea that he get them from your computer. And he fought me hard on it, but it was the only way."

"But you could have just asked me. You could have told me—"

"And risk your getting fired if John found out?" David's face grew hard. "No way. I'd rather go to jail for theft than have you fired for helping me."

Kim nodded, pieces of the last few weeks falling into place. "That's why you've been so helpful this whole time. That's why I kept finding you poking around in places you shouldn't be."

Dave sighed as he sat down on the edge of his desk. "No one knows I'm anything more than manager of the spa there."

"It gave you the perfect cover to investigate," she said softly. "And our friendship—"

"I didn't want to do it. I swear to you, I never would have if John hadn't been lying to us."

Carl leaned forward. "I made him do it. Don't be angry with Dave. I made him—"

"I'm still an adult, Uncle Carl," David interrupted, but his gaze remained on Kim. "I made that choice knowing I was abusing your trust." He leaned forward, his expression anguished. "I'm so sorry. But…"

"You needed the proof," she said softly. "Damn it, David, why didn't you tell me? Why didn't you just ask? I would have done it for you."

"No way. John's a lot more of an ass than you know. I just didn't want you mixed up in it. This was my risk to take."

He sighed. "I can still be brought up on charges."

She abruptly shot to her feet. "Not going to happen. John was falsifying records. He doesn't have to know how you got the proof."

David straightened up, grabbing her hands. "This is messy stuff. I won't put you at risk."

She snorted. "My desk, my account. I'm already—"

"No." He said the word softly. "We don't have to purchase the club, Kim. We can just say no to the deal and all of this disappears."

"And let John get away with this?" She snorted. "Hell no! Plus, I *want* you to buy the club. John's bleeding it dry. It could be so much more if he'd just invest a little money." She fell silent, her mind racing back over all the years of complaining she'd done to David. How many times had she said that if she were owner, she'd stop being so pinchpenny with everything there. That the club could be something special with just a small investment of capital. And she could do it. If she just had the means.

She looked at him, her brows coming together. It wasn't possible. He couldn't possibly have gotten the idea to buy the club from her.

Meanwhile, David flashed her one of those amazing smiles of his. "Did I ever tell you how I got started in the spa business?"

She shook her head. No, she'd never asked.

"My uncle's fault. He gave me my first job as a teenager."

Carl laughed. "I was just being nice. Put him in charge of janitorial, but he took right to it. By the time the summer was out, he knew about every aspect of the business."

"Best damn summer job I ever had."

"Within a year, he was running the place. Way better than I did, by the way. We bought our second property while he was in college."

"I didn't have any money, but I had sweat equity. Plus a generous profit-sharing package."

His uncle shrugged. "He's family. Plus, he was worth the risk. He bought into ownership the year he graduated from college. Then he spearheaded the purchase of the next three properties."

Kim smiled, seeing David in a whole new light. "And now you want to buy John's Fitness. Why?"

He was still holding her hands, which he now drew up to his lips, pressing a kiss there. "Because I see the potential in it. And I know this amazing manager who hasn't been allowed to make the club into what it could be."

She swallowed. "Me?"

He nodded. "You."

She closed her eyes a moment, blocking out the sight of him looking all sweet and charming in front of her. But it didn't stop her from feeling his hands holding hers or the memory of the way he was looking at her with hope and... and something else shining through his eyes.

"God, everything is happening so fast." They'd only started their romantic relationship a few days ago.

"You've known me for three years," he said. "And I've known exactly what I want for almost as long."

Kim's eyes snapped open and she stared at him. He didn't mean... He couldn't possibly...

"I love you, Kim. I have for a very long time."

"I..." She was about to say that she was at a loss. That everything was moving too fast. But even though her brain said those things, her heart was telling her something entirely different. Sure, their romance had just started, but she'd loved David for a very long time. He was her best friend, after all. "I love you, too," she whispered. Then she laughed. "Oh my God, we're in love!"

She might have said more, but there wasn't time. Suddenly, David was right there, kissing her as if she was the answer to his prayer. And maybe she was, because he damn sure was the answer to hers.

Meanwhile, behind her, Carl cleared his throat. "Well, I think I'll just…um…go do some paperwork or something."

Neither David nor Kim responded. They were too busy celebrating.

Epilogue

Kim cheered with everyone else when the new sign went up. John's Fitness was now Kim's Health Club and Spa. She was a subsidiary of Pamper Me Spa, but the profit-sharing terms were very generous. She was, after all, family now.

It had been a long haul to get here. Turns out the purchase of the health club had been the easiest part. After confronting John with his lies, they were able to buy the club for a song. But a thorough accounting audit along with a mound of paperwork had delayed things nearly a year. Long enough for her to fall even more deeply in love with David. Long enough for him to propose and for them to marry. And now she had finally claimed the club as her own.

She smiled at her new husband, wondering if David knew just how happy he'd made her. One year ago, she'd lost her pro career, thought she was going crazy, and been so twisted around she hadn't even realized how lonely she was. All it had taken was one man—and one incredible night—to show her how different things could be.

David lifted her hand, kissing the wedding ring on her finger. "Have I told you lately how amazing you are? How happy you make me?"

She grinned. "Yes," she said, "but I never tire of hearing it." She pressed a hot kiss to his lips. "Especially since the feeling is very mutual."

"Good," he said, his blue eyes sparkling in the sunlight. "Because I've set you up with a very special relaxation package at the spa. Exclusive pampering time given to you by a very handsome godlike man."

"Hmm, definitely godlike. But…" She bit her lip and gestured to the club.

"But you have a ton of work," he finished for her.

She shrugged. "We've just started on the renovations. Plus the new Jacuzzi is getting installed today and—"

He pressed a finger to her lips, cutting off her words. "I know," he said. Then he replaced his fingers with his lips. One quick kiss later, he was pulling back. "That's why I've set up your appointment for after close."

"When we have the entire floor to ourselves?"

He grinned. "Yup."

"You are the best husband ever."

His expression sobered a bit. "What about best friend? Do I still have that title?"

"You bet," she said with a laugh. "And the best godlike lover one, too."

He grinned. "Well, that one I already knew."

She punched him lightly on the arm. He caught it, of course, easily swinging her into his arms. And when they finally separated—amid hoots and cheers from their employees—he whispered the words she never tired of hearing. "I love you."

"Right back atcha, godman."

He stroked her cheek, tenderness and love in the caress. Then together, they walked into her new club.

About the Author

Kathy Lyons is the fun, contemporary side of USA Today Bestselling author Jade Lee. She loves sassy romance with lots of laughter and sex. Spice is the variety of life, right? Okay, so maybe two kids, two cats, two pennames, and writing over 40 books has messed with her mind, but she still keeps having fun.

Check her out at www.KathyLyons.com.

Or hang out with her sexy historical half, Jade Lee. Titled heroes with dark secrets are Jade's passion. Especially when they fall for women who add more than just spice to their lives.

Find her at www.JadeLeeAuthor.com
Facebook: JadeLeeBooks
Twitter: JadeLeeAuthor

www.ingramcontent.com/pod-product-compliance
Lightning Source LLC
Chambersburg PA
CBHW022041170626
46808CB00003B/1304